PLAYBOY'S HIDEAWAY

The kitchen had a freezer, the bathroom plumbing was made of gold, and the bedroom ceiling was solid mirror. There was no telephone. It would have been corny, if the hideaway hadn't become a hideout.

Holed up in his private orgy-pad, a millionaire playboy hires Peter Chambers to find out who murdered his ex-ladylove. Not that the millionaire really cares, but the cops have tagged him killer. When Chambers crashes into an unsavory nightworld of junkies, gigolos and dancehall girls, he finds someone has tagged _him_ . . . as the next victim.

And that someone could be any of a number of would-be playmates. Including a man-hunting amazon who is too delicious not to be deadly.

Death is the Last Lover

Henry Kane

Adams Media

New York London Toronto Sydney New Delhi

Published in electronic format by
PROLOGUE BOOKS
an imprint of F+W Media, Inc.
10151 Carver Road
Blue Ash, Ohio 45242
www.prologuebooks.com

eISBN 10: 1-4405-3907-3
eISBN 13: 978-1-4405-3907-7
POD ISBN 10: 1-4405-5623-7
POD ISBN 13: 978-1-4405-5623-4

This is a work of fiction. Names, characters, corporations, institutions,
organizations, events, or locales in this novel are either the product of the author's
imagination or, if real, used fictitiously. The resemblance of any character to actual
persons (living or dead) is entirely coincidental.

This work has been previously published in print format by:
Signet Books, The New American Library, Inc., New York, NY.

ONE

I was lying around the house like a lox.

Lying around the house like a lox!

For the outlanders: explanation.

House, in the seaport town of New York, is colloquial for abode, any abode, be it a one-room folding apartment near the Battery or a glass mansion on the very easterly edge of the chic East Side. Lox, in the seaport town of New York, is colloquial for smoked salmon. Smoked salmon, in the seaport town of New York, lies about in shameless display, belly-side up and inert, in the front windows of the appetizing stores. An appetizing store, in the seaport town of New York, is not at all a store that is appetizing. Appetizing store, in the seaport town of New York, is a store that trades in a type of comestible which purports to give one an appetite for the further comestibles of a civilized meal. Generally, it does not give one an appetite. Generally, it gives one heartburn in the schmaltz region. Heartburn in the schmaltz region, in the seaport town of New York—

Oh no!

Please!

Let us start all over again.

Me, I was lying around the house (which is a three-room apartment with a terrace on Central Park South) like a smoked salmon in an appetizing store, belly-side up and inert. I was lying around like a smoked salmon because I was bored. Even private detectives—and all you *aficionados* may now rise in high dudgeon and scoff in low moans—get bored. I was bored with skip tracings, and bill collectings, and tracking erring husbands, and untracking erring wives—I was bored with the routine of my racket. Nothing of real interest had happened for months, and I'd had it—right up to the gullet. So this day I had packed up and gone home. I had

5

told my secretary that I was going to lazy the day, that I would be at home, and that I was not to be disturbed unless it was something special.

Turned out it was something extra, *extra* special.

I was lying around, in comfortable briefs, lapping up the scandal of the tabloids—when the bell rang. Unthinking, I shoved out from beneath the newspapers, crawled off the couch, ambled to the door, opened it, and felt myself grow reverently rigid at the pulchritude so unexpectedly delineated in my doorway.

"Mr. Chambers?" she inquired.

"Mr. Chambers," I replied.

"I am Sophia Sierra," she declared.

Sophia Sierra, so help me. That was the name.

"Please come in," I said. She crossed the threshold, and I closed the door, but I held on to the knob for succor. "I don't quite understand . . ." I began.

"The lady in your office," said Sophia Sierra. "She told me I would find you here."

"Yes, yes," I mumbled. "The lady in my office . . ."

Ah, secretaries. Ah, the impishness in the impish hearts of the ladies of the office in all the offices all over the world. Ah, the devious twists in the peculiar psyches of staid secretaries. Ah, ah, ah. A hunk of stuff turns up that is enough to rock you on your heels and start you talking to yourself, but the lady of your office, in perverse abandon, and knowing full well it *is* perverse abandon, does not even lift a finger to ring you on the phone in order to warn you of the impending onslaught of an emotional blockbuster. But she had *not* sent her away! She *had* sent her through! And just for that, if for nothing else, the lady of the office was entitled to a substantial increase in salary come Christmas (triggered now, but an increase which had been scatteringly contemplated prior to now).

And suddenly, hanging on to a doorknob and ogling a Sophia Sierra, I realized I was utterly unclad except for the skimpiest of shorts.

"Forgive me," I said, relinquishing the doorknob and making a grotesque effort at a gentlemanly bow. "I . . . I didn't expect company. I . . . I'll go . . . make myself presentable."

"You're presentable," she said. "Quite presentable. Quite, indeed."

"I am?" I said like an oaf, and I stood there, and we ogled

one another, and I do not know what thoughts she had, but the thoughts I had might make themselves too obviously apparent, so I waved her to the living room, scampered to the bedroom, donned a T-shirt, slacks, socks and loafers, and scampered back to the living room—but not before I had had a fast glance at the mirror and a fast comb at the hair.

She was out on the terrace.

It was warm for the time of year and she had removed her coat. She was leaning on the balustrade—elbows resting and hands clasped—looking out upon the city: which gave me a moment to look out upon her.

She was something to look out upon.

Her close-fitting dress was black, her high-heeled pumps were black, her stockings were the sheerest of jet black nylon. Her flesh was cream-soft white, the dress so cut that much of the cream-soft whiteness was enticingly exposed. It was a sleeveless, clinging, knitted black dress, cut deep in front, deep in back, and deep at the arms.

She turned, suddenly, from the balustrade, and paced slowly, regarding me. She regarded me—I regarded her.

I insist: she was something to be regarded.

Black and white. That was the picture. Flesh white, all else black. Her hair was curl-heavy black worn long behind small ears and falling below the nape of the neck; eyes wide and black, so black the pupils merged with the irises; eyebrows black and bold and long; black and white—except for the glistening red of a pouting full-lipped mouth. She was tall, with an absurdly exaggerated figure, but not too absurd not to be taken most seriously: protruding breasts; tiny cinched-in waist; firm, round, ungirdled buttocks; long powerful strong thighs; sturdy calves and slender ankles. Snap judgment, she was either a neck-moving elbow-pointing modern-type dancer, or a rump-moving nipple-pointing specialty-type stripper, or a showgirl with Cadillacs waiting at the stage-door.

"I'm a messenger," she said.

"Messengers like this," I said, "should happen to me the rest of my life. Your name really Sophia Sierra?"

"Sophia Sierra," she said. "I'm Cuban."

"But you speak English perfectly."

"Oh, I was born here. I mean I'm of Cuban extraction."

"Like a drink?" I said, touching her elbow, moving her back to the living room.

"No, thank you." And in the living room she stood stock-still, long-fingered hands on her hips, eyes moving over me. "I've heard about you," she said. She had a voice that came from deep in her throat, soft, smooth and pitched low.

"So?" I said.

"Heard you're kind of a ladies' man."

"So?" I said.

"Nothing," she said, "except that, kind of, I can understand it." Her smile showed high square teeth and there was suddenly a curiously wicked expression around her eyes. Almost defiantly, she strode to me, moved close. "I eat ladykillers," she said. Her face was inches away from mine, but parts of her were touching me; she was built like that.

"I'm willing to be devoured," I said.

"Crazy, huh?" she said.

"What's crazy?" I said.

"People going for people, bang, just like that."

"What's crazy about it?" I said. "Happens all the time."

I reached for her. She moved away.

"I'm a messenger," she said.

"I got that message. I'm getting other messages."

"Skip that for now, will you?"

"Only if you promise a raincheck."

"I promise," she said. "I'm really here with a message."

"From whom?" I said.

"George Phillips," she said.

"Who?" I said.

"George Phillips," she said.

"I don't know any George Phillips," I said.

She went to her handbag, took out a yellow sheet of paper, and brought it to me. It was a telegram addressed to S. SIERRA, 11 EAST 45th STREET. It said: PLEASE CONTACT PETER CHAMBERS AT ONCE. HAVE HIM GET IN TOUCH WITH ME. TELL HIM WHERE. I MUST SEE HIM IMMEDIATELY. HE IS A FRIEND. G. PHILLIPS.

"Maybe I *am* a friend of G. Phillips," I said, "but you wouldn't know it from me. Honest, I never heard of a G. Phillips in my life."

"Ever hear of a Gordon Phelps?"

"Gordon Phelps I heard of."

"George Phillips is Gordon Phelps."

"Gordon Phelps!" I brushed past her and lifted one of

the tabloids, turned to page three, and pointed. *"This* Gordon Phelps?" I said.

"That's the one," she said.

The prize item on page three had to do with the death of Vivian Frayne. Vivian Frayne had been a hostess in a dance hall called the Nirvana Ballroom. There was a photo of Vivian Frayne, a theatrical photo of a lush blonde revealingly swathed in diaphanous veils. Vivian Frayne had been murdered. She had been found early this morning in her two-room apartment attired in lounging pajamas. Five bullets had penetrated the lounging pajamas, indenting Vivian Frayne. Three of the bullets, although lodged in attractive sites, had been of no lethal consequence, but either of the other two— one just above the heart and the other in the region of the stomach—had served as the proximate cause of her decease. A gun had been found on the premises but the newspaper did not elaborate on its significance, merely making the bald statement: "A gun was discovered in the apartment." The last paragraph reported: "The police are seeking one Gordon Phelps, millionaire playboy, in connection with their investigation."

"Gordon Phelps," I said, laying away the paper, "is G. Phillips?"

"Uh, huh," said Sophia Sierra.

"And he sent you to contact me?"

"Just like it says in the telegram."

"I don't get it."

"Why not?"

"Couldn't he contact me himself?"

"Cops are looking for him. You just read it in the paper, didn't you?"

"He could have called me on the phone, couldn't he? I'm in the book, both office and home."

"He couldn't have called you."

"Why not?" I said.

"He's got no phone."

"Gordon Phelps? No phone? Gordon Phelps owns a thirty-room mansion on Fifth Avenue. Thirty-room mansions generally have phones."

"If the cops are looking for him," she said, "he doesn't figure to be in his thirty-room mansion, does he?"

"Check," I said. "But there are phones *outside* of thirty-room mansions."

"There's no phone where he is."

"Where the hell is he?"

"In a little hideaway he's got—that only a few of his intimate friends know about."

"You one of his intimate friends?"

"Let's say I'm one of his . . . good friends."

"Okay, good friend, so where's this hideaway?"

"Down in the village. 11 Charles Street. Apartment 2A. He's listed as G. Phillips. And that's where you're supposed to go."

"Okay, I'm going," I said. "So how come there's no phone there?"

"Because it's a hideaway."

"Hideaways can't have phones?"

"Not this hideaway."

"All right," I said, "the hell with it. Now what about—our raincheck?"

She went for her coat, slung it over one shoulder.

"I'd like," she said, "if you'd like."

"I like, I like," I said. "How about this evening?"

"I'm working this evening."

"All right. How about after work?"

"How about *during* work?" she said.

I lifted my eyebrows for her. "What kind of work do you do?"

"Just like Vivian Frayne," she said.

"Pardon?" I said.

"I'm a hostess at the Nirvana Ballroom."

"I'll be there," I said. "That's a wild business, isn't it?"

"You have your freedom," she said.

"What's that mean?"

"Once you're a regular, it's kind of like piece-work. You show up whenever you feel like it. You throw on an evening gown and you're working—at fifty percent of whatever the suckers contribute. I mean, you've got anything else to do, you just don't show up."

"I'll be there," I said.

"Swell," she said. "For you I'll wear my red gown."

"Special, the red gown?"

"Wait'll you see me in it. You'll die."

"I'm dying right now," I said.

She smiled her wicked smile, waved, went to the door and opened it.

"I'm looking forward," she said.

"I'll cancel the G. Phillips if you say so."

"I'm not saying so. Bye, now. I'm looking forward."

She was already outside the door when I called, "Oh! About Vivian Frayne. Did you know her? Vivian Frayne."

She stuck her head back.

"I knew her," she said.

And she closed her door behind her.

And I was left with the faint musk of her perfume.

TWO

I undressed, showered, and re-dressed for Gordon Phelps. Gordon Phelps was not a friend. The term "friend" is tossed about as loosely as shredded lettuce in a salad pot. Gordon Phelps was an acquaintance, a guy I'd run into in the night clubs, a guy with more loot than he could possibly spend, and a guy for whom I had done a few favors, for a fee. He was a sixty-year-old runabout who still had plenty of vitamins jiggling inside of him. He had, I had heard, an austere society-type wife who kept a rather slack rein on him. I had not heard as to what rein he kept on her. He had, aside from a society-type wife, a fabulous town house on Fifth Avenue, a fabulous beach house on Fire Island, and a fabulous country house in Palm Beach—but I had never heard of his having a hideaway which, of course, is the basic meaning of hideaway—you are not supposed to hear of it. The fact that the cops were looking for *him* coupled with the fact that he was looking for *me* spelled out a simple equation with a single solution: business. For me. And since Gordon Phelps was inordinately generous in the matter of fees (he could afford it) I was quite as anxious to see Gordon Phelps as Gordon Phelps was to see me.

THREE

The cab delivered me to 11 Charles Street which was a new house in an old neighborhood, a squat, wide, five-story job on a clean quiet street in Greenwich Village. In the lobby, a neat bracket alongside a neat button showed me G. PHILLIPS. I pushed at the neat button alongside the neat bracket and received a quick click in response. Inside, a plush elevator, push-button style, lifted me to 2, and at the door marked A, I applied pressure to another neat button. The mirror of a mirror-faced peekhole disappeared and a blinking eye replaced it. Then the round mirror fell back and the door swung open.

"Hail and welcome," Gordon Phelps said. "And it's about time."

"I made it as soon as I could, Mr. Phelps."

"What held you up?" he said. "The sultry Sierra?"

"No, but she could have, if she'd had a mind to."

"Terrific piece, that one, eh?"

"Yes, sir, Mr. Phelps."

"But you just look out there, sonny."

"Because why, Mr. Phelps?"

"Because she's exactly the opposite of what she looks like. That little gal is all mind and no heart, and it's a mind concerned with one thing—gold, pure and simple. Gold, gelt, loot, dinero. But come on now, make yourself to home, young fella. We've got a hell of a lot of talking to do."

He led me through a small round foyer into an enormous exquisitely furnished living room, its floor moss-soft with thick rose-colored carpeting. Rose-colored drapes covered all of the walls from floor to ceiling, slit for windows at one wall, and cut out for a gold fireplace at another. Above the fireplace hung a huge oil of a rose-colored nude, the only picture in the room. A rose-colored ceiling sprouted an antique gold chandelier, warm light pouring from its crystals.

12

The furniture—desk, chairs, couches, tables, bar, lamps, hassocks—was all black. The wood was ebony, the fabrics and adornments all gold. That was the room: rose and black and gold in such artistic ensemble as to take your breath away.

"Just beautiful," I said.

"Would you like to see more?" He had a cultured, somewhat high-pitched voice, like a coloratura soprano who drank too much. "And by the way, that fireplace really burns wood."

"Love to see more," I said.

He motioned me to a bedroom which was bleak compared to the dazzlements of the living room. The ceiling was all mirror. One wall was all mirror. The other walls were papered green and there was a green carpet. There was a large walnut four-poster, a walnut dresser, two walnut bed-tables, two lamps with green silk shades—and nothing else, not even a picture on a wall.

He showed me a bathroom with gold plumbing, and a kitchen with all the equipment including a deep-freeze, and back once again in the living room he made drinks.

"I could live here for months," he said, "without going out once. There's enough food and drink—for months."

"Is that the way you'd like it?" I said.

"Pardon?"

"Not going out for months."

"That's the way I'd hate it," he said. "That's why you're here."

"Why am I here, Mr. Phelps?"

He paced with light steps. He was tall and slender and rather graceful, muscular for his age. He had white wispy hair neatly parted in the middle, a pink face, and a delicate nose.

"I want to get out of here," he said, "and I want to get out of here soon. And I want *you* to get me out of here." He went to his desk, brought out an oblong metal box, extracted a number of bills, counted them and brought them to me. "Here," he said. "Money of the realm."

I counted the money of the realm. It amounted to five thousand dollars. I pocketed the money of the realm, sighed, squirmed, took up my drink.

"Whom did you murder?" I said.

"I didn't murder anyone," he said.

"Five thousand bucks is a lot of money for not murdering anyone, not even Vivian Frayne."

"I did not murder Vivian Frayne."

"Do you know who did?"

"No."

"Then why are you holed up?"

"Because, a little bit, I'm mixed up in it."

"And you want me to un-mix?"

"Precisely."

I sighed again. "Sit down," I said, "won't you? Refill our glasses, please, and sit down. Let's talk up a little storm, huh? But I'm telling you right now, any way it turns out, I keep the fee."

"Any way it turns out," he said, "you keep the fee."

"I mean even if it turns out you."

He had blue eyes and they grew narrow as he smiled, sadly. He shrugged, lifted the glasses, brought them to the bar, re-filled them, came back and sat down beside me.

"Drink hearty," he said and he handed me my glass.

"*A vôtre santé,*" I said.

"I'm ready for the inquisition," he said.

"Good," I said. "Let's start with right here. What's with a hideaway? What's with no phone?"

Demurely he said, "Hideaway? Let's call it . . . retreat. Doesn't sound so . . . er . . . quite so illicit" He smiled his sad smile again.

"Okay," I said. "Retreat. So why a retreat without a phone?"

"That's the point of a retreat, isn't it?"

"Is it?"

"I mean," he said, "somewhere to get away, to be alone without risk of outside interference."

"Alone?" I said, subtle as a spanking in the woodshed.

"Either alone, or with very special company."

"And a phone spoils that?"

"A phone is a means of communication with the outside world. Here, I prefer to be out of communication."

"Suppose you got sick?"

"I could always crawl out and knock on a neighbor's door, or go out into the hall and yell. If you're too sick to do any of that, you'd be too sick to use the phone, wouldn't you?"

"The rich," I said, "can afford to be eccentric."

"All right," he said, "let's leave it at that."

I cast my eyes about the room, let them rest for a moment

on the rose-colored nude, brought them back to him. "Who, please," I said, "knows about this place?"

He shrugged, delicately. "Not too many."

"How many, Mr. Phelps?"

"I don't quite know, Mr. Chambers, but those who do, they know me as George Phillips, not Gordon Phelps. I had my attorney—whom I trust implicitly—find this place for me, arrange for the lease and all that. I used a decorator to furnish—as George Phillips, of course—and I paid him in cash."

"Does your wife know?"

"No, and she wouldn't like it if she did. Matter of fact, I think she'd hate it. There's a thing called . . . over-stepping the bounds."

"I've heard," I said.

"It's a relative term, of course. There's a good deal of overstepping bounds that my wife forgives, as long as such activity is discreet. This sort of thing isn't exactly discreet. If it were found out, my wife's friends might giggle at her. My wife doesn't like to be giggled at."

"That all you're worried about—that she might be giggled at?"

"When she's giggled at—when she's made a show of—she can become quite fierce."

"And you're afraid of her when she's quite fierce?"

He pinched the point of his nose. "Not afraid, physically. But you see, my wife controls with me, jointly, a good deal of my . . . er . . . how shall I say . . . my fortune. Her becoming fierce could prove embarrassing to me, quite embarrassing. As is, we have rather a harmonious relationship—she understands my quirks, I understand hers. Quite harmonious. But I don't think she would approve of anything quite so uncircumspect as a . . . er . . . a retreat."

"Then why do you do it, Mr. Phelps?"

The blue eyes regarded me steadily but reprovingly. One eyebrow arched and a latticework of fine wrinkles appeared on his forehead. "Why do any of us do any of the things we shouldn't do, Mr. Chambers?" Now the eyes studied me, despairingly. "We have needs, compulsions, desires——"

"Speaking of desires," I said. "How about Sophia Sierra?"

"Yes?" he said.

"She knows that the George Phillips with the hideaway is the Gordon Phelps with the retreat."

"Yes," he said.

"Doesn't that worry you?"

"No."

"Why not?"

"I think," he said, "the word is empirical."

"I beg your pardon?"

"She's known for some time that George Phillips is Gordon Phelps. She's done nothing about it, made no threat or suggestion of threat. I admit, at the beginning, I was worried. Now—empirically—I'm not worried about Sophia. It was Vivian Frayne I was worried about."

"Let's finish Sophia first. Who told her? You?"

"Of course not."

"Do you know who?"

"Yes. Steve Pedi."

"Who?" I said.

"Steve Pedi."

"And who in hell is Steve Pedi?"

"Steve Pedi owns the Nirvana Ballroom."

"And did you tell Steve Pedi?"

"No, I did not."

"Then who, please, told Steve Pedi?"

He raised both hands at me like a symphony conductor trying to hold down the kettle-drums. "Look, please, Mr. Chambers," he said, "let's do it right side up, shall we? Let's try to do it—one thing at a time."

"Yes, yes," I said. "It began with Sophia Sierra. It's just that I was interested in Sophia Sierra."

The eyebrows came down in narrow crags above the blue eyes that suddenly twinkled. *"Were* interested—or *are* interested?"

"Is that a crack, Mr. Phelps?"

"It is that, Mr. Chambers. Precisely."

A chuckle rumbled out of me—there was something about the man, almost a childish directness, a sort of winning wistfulness, a naive-naughty little-boy attitude which, in its innocent astonishment, makes a knave of an attempted critic. I was reminded of the story of the kid who had urinated in mama's wash because he had heard that an acid content makes the clothes whiter. Poor Mama. Poor me. I liked the guy. I could not help myself. I would hate it if it turned out that he had murdered Vivian Frayne.

"Did you?" I said.

"What?"

"Kill her?" I said.

"No. But let me tell you something. In the interests of self-preservation—*my* self-preservation—I'm going to do my darndest to implicate anybody with the slightest reason to have wanted her dead."

"Did *you* want her dead, Mr. Phelps?"

He leaned forward. A parched smile came to his face, and went away. For the first time, his eyes avoided mine as he said, slowly, "Yes. Yes, Mr. Chambers. Yes, I think I did."

FOUR

I refilled my own glass. I sipped and set it away. I lit a cigarette and walked around a bit. He remained where he was, seated quietly, his hands together, palm to palm, between his knees. I smiled at him, tentatively, and he returned the smile. The only show of his nervousness was the pressure of his knees on his hands. They were tight together, like a frightened virgin's. I sat down near him. I said, "Let's begin at the beginning, shall we?"

His knees eased up. He rubbed his palms together. "At the beginning," he said, "there is I."

"Very Biblical," I said, "but I don't get it."

"I must explain myself to you first. I mean, a little bit about myself."

"Sure," I said. "Explain."

He grabbed at his drink, gulped, put it aside. He ran the point of a fingernail through his hair.

"We're all human," he said. "Let's put it that way, we're all human."

"Fair enough," I said. "At the beginning there are always platitudes."

"I like girls," he said.

"Hooray for you," I said.

"I like girls who are young, strong, beautiful, vital."

"You're not alone," I said.

"I don't like the people in my own sphere. I don't like

the thinking ones, the cerebral ones, the mush-mouthed ones with their stiff fathers and mothers. I—how shall I put it—I seek out, sort of, the lower depths, the physical, passionate people of a world other than my own. Perhaps I have a need to feel superior, perhaps my emotions need the whip of—"

"Okay," I said, "with the abnormal psychology. I dig. Let's move it from there."

"I am a frequenter of dance halls—low, cheap, masturbation types of dance hall. In such environment, I am most superior."

"Like how, Mr. Phelps?"

"There are few millionaires in cheap dime-a-dance places."

"How about the girls, Mr. Phelps?"

"Surprisingly beautiful, sir. Kids earning a living—kids without any special talent, except youth and beauty. An old bird like myself, I'm a character in dance halls. I get acquainted with charming young girls, I move slowly, I don't frighten them. But most of all in my favor, I have a good deal of money to throw around—and basically these kids have one prime need: money." His smile was momentary. "Like that, and in that element, I can compete with my younger brethren."

"What's wrong," I said, "with call-girls?"

"Nothing, except they're not for me. My needs involve an emotional entanglement—I can't just be *buying* a body. If it is a purchase, purely a purchase, I have no reaction, no feeling, no desire—quite the contrary, I'm repelled."

"I dig," I said. "Get off the couch, Mr. Phelps. I'm not here as a psychoanalyst."

"The hell with you," he said.

"Mutual," I said. "I take it you hit the Nirvana Ballroom in your quest for non-call-girl call-girls."

"It was about six months ago. I went there as George Phillips, of course."

"But of course."

"Originally, I was attracted to Sophia Sierra."

"I cannot blame you in the least," I said.

"But that one was too coldly mercenary for me. She was right on top of the ball all the time."

"What did you expect? That she'd fall in love with you? Why, you can be her father, for Chrissake."

"I smell maleness," he said, "and I smell youth, and male

ego, and a definite interest in Sophia Sierra. I smell Peter
Chambers on the hunt, and I warn Peter Chambers right now.
Take it from an old friend, Peter—not your youth, nor your
maleness, nor your definite interest will carry you one whit
with Sophia Sierra. That one, at this moment in her life, is
whore, all whore, period."

"Thanks, Dad," I said. "I got you off the couch, now come
off the lecture platform. What happened with Sophia Sierra?"

"I took her out, showed her the good side of town. I
bought her a few frocks, a few dinners, lent her a little money
on long-term loans, if you know what I mean. I let her know
that papa was well-heeled and charitably inclined."

"Did you make it?"

"No."

"Could you have?"

"Honestly, I'm not sure. I got close, but I didn't get where
I wanted to get. A peculiar girl, straightforward on one hand,
conniving on another."

"Let's start with straightforward," I said.

"She told me, quite quickly, that she knew I was Gordon
Phelps."

"And she told you *how* she knew?"

"She told me that Steve Pedi had informed her."

"And she told you how Steve Pedi knew. I mean, did she
know that?"

"Steve Pedi, it appears, is a rather bright young man."

"Did he name that place Nirvana?"

"Yes, he did."

"Then he's a rather imaginative young man too, wouldn't
you say?"

"Yes, I would say."

"All right. How did he know George Phillips was Gordon
Phelps?"

"Simple enough. Seems he has a little staff there at the
Nirvana, some of whom serve as investigators. Any . . . er
. . . unusual patron—he finds out who he is. He found out
who I was, and he informed Sophia."

"Why?" I said.

"Why not? He likes Sophia. Why shouldn't he . . . er . . .
steer her to a good thing?"

"Meaning—you're the good thing."

"For Sophia—I was a good thing."

"Did he also inform Vivian Frayne?"

"He did not inform Vivian Frayne."

"Why? Didn't he like Vivian Frayne?"

"No, it appears he did not like Vivian Frayne."

"Okay," I said. "Are we finished with Sophia?"

"I am finished with the straightforward."

I tried to keep the edge out of my voice. "Proceed then, please, with the conniving."

"The conniving involved a lalapaloosa."

"Lalapaloosa?" I inquired.

Quiver of muscles at the hinge of the jaw betrayed emotion but his tone remained as level as anchovies in a tin. "Have you ever heard of Elia Strassan?"

"Why should I be an exception?" I said. "Elia Strassan. Probably the greatest dramatic coach produced in America. Guy was in his prime about ten years ago, then he got sick and retired." I had displayed knowledge of my client, now I displayed bewilderment. "What earthly connection between Strassan and Sierra?"

"This was Sophia's lalapaloosa," Gordon Phelps said. "She propositioned me." Mockery clouded his eyes. "Seems she wants to be a great dramatic actress. Seems she wants to study with Strassan."

"But he's not having any," I said. "Or is he?"

"Private tutorship, Sophia told me. Told me that Strassan wanted ten thousand dollars—in advance—for a year's private tutorship. Asked to borrow the money from me. You know what I mean—borrow."

"Did you give it to her?"

"I checked."

"Whom?"

"Strassan."

"How?"

"I hired a peeper."

"I don't remember the assignment."

He grinned embarrassedly. "I wouldn't have the nerve to bother you with that kind of assignment. That's chicken feed for you."

"Whom did you use?"

"Guy my wife uses on occasion."

"Who?"

"Si Murray."

"Si Murray's a crook."

"This was nothing. A little matter. Nothing fiduciary."

"Okay," I said. "So?"

"First, Strassan wasn't teaching any more. He'd had a stroke and was confined to a chair. But, it seems, little Sophia had gotten to him, made him happy right there in his chair. Because Strassan verified for her, said he'd be willing to take her on, privately, for a year, for ten thousand. He needs ten thousand like he needs ten thousand holes in his head—the guy is independently wealthy. Si Murray checked some more for me. Dear Sophia had pulled this thing before. Grabbed a few suckers on this deal—seems there are others like me who look for kicks in dance halls. Each time Strassan covered for her. Oh, I'm certain that kid can make an old man happy right there in his wheel chair." Gordon Phelps stood up, paced, kicked at the carpet, came back, flung himself down. "That baby doesn't want to be an actress. All she wants is to garner a great big bankroll while she's young enough and beautiful enough to garner same. That's all that's on her mind—money, important money. And she uses that dance hall as a base of operations. Men come, and she sifts through them. She discards the little fish and tries to hook the big ones. Strange little whore, that kid, but all whore."

"Did you give her the money?"

"No, sir. I passed."

"To Vivian Frayne?" I said.

"Yes. She had been making overtures, and I was interested. Quite another type, Vivian Frayne. A blonde, older and softer than the sprightly Sophia. About thirty, I'd say, but quite lovely. Kind of a schizo. All soft on one side, all hard on the other. Queer dame, but we made out well."

I said: "So Sophia got the air."

"She did," he said.

I said: "How did she take it?"

"Like unto burst with anger," he said. "Somehow, she didn't blame me. She blamed Vivian. Hated her guts, at having lost her prize fish to Vivian. But she stayed along with me, she did, as kind of a lost friend."

"And you and Vivian?"

"Went along for months, and most satisfactorily."

"Now hold it," I said.

"Yes, please?" he said.

"Did Vivian know you were Gordon Phelps?"

"Yes."

"Pedi tell her?"

"No, Pedi did not tell her."

"How do you know that?"

"She and Pedi were not on the best of terms. Pedi was not going to steer a sucker to Vivian Frayne."

"Well, then, who the hell did tell her?"

I tapped out my cigarette and Gordon Phelps lit one. "That was a great big secret," he said. "She knew who I was, but she insisted she was honor-bound not to tell me how she knew."

"Queer characters, these chicks," I said.

"What do you expect?" said Gordon Phelps.

"Okay," I said. "How did it go—you and Vivian Frayne?"

"Excellently, for a while," he said. "But suddenly she began to swing the big bat too, looking for a home run."

"Like how?" I said.

"Like a sudden interest in travel. Wanted two years in Europe, felt it would broaden her. Tell you the truth, I was ready. I'd have been glad to get rid of her, if the request were within reason. I was ready to move on to greener pastures, or should I say blonder?"

"How much," I said, "to broaden herself in Europe?"

"A hundred thousand dollars."

"Wow," I said. "You realized, I trust, the trip to Europe was strictly confetti? You realized, I trust, that the hundred thousand dollars was a straight hold-up?"

"Of course I did. To be absolutely honest, I'd have paid it if I hadn't realized just that. The little lady had me where the hair is short. She could have caused me a good deal of inconvenience, a *good* deal of inconvenience. But it was straight blackmail, no matter how she put it. And you know about blackmail—once begun, it never ends. It posed a problem, all right. Believe me, it posed a problem."

"When did she make this play?"

"About two weeks ago."

"And what did you tell her?"

"Told her I wanted to think about it."

"And how did she take that?"

"She was most gracious."

"And how did it finally resolve itself?"

"You know how. She died."

"I know she was murdered," I said.

"Yes," he said, "she was murdered." And the blue eyes moved to mine, pleadingly.

FIVE

Now I was up and pacing. I helped myself to more of his whiskey, neat, one drink and slam of glass. "Look," I said, "did you kill her? Because if you did, I'm the man to talk to. There are all kinds of crazy angles, you know, legal angles. Justifiable homicide, self-defense, even insanity, temporary insanity. You were a guy very much in the middle, and a guy very much in the middle can go out of his mind—"

"I didn't kill her," he said.

"When did you find out about it?"

"About nine o'clock this morning."

"How?"

"It came in over the radio."

"What came in? I only read a half-ass newspaper account."

"She was found at seven this morning. Time of death was estimated for one o'clock last night. There was the usual sensational blasting, and then the fact that the police were looking for me—Gordon Phelps."

"Any ideas why?"

"I assume she had mentioned my real name to some of her friends, and the police had questioned these friends."

"Mr. Phelps," I said, "if the police were looking for you—and you had nothing to do with it—why in thunder are you holed up here? Why didn't you go down and talk to them?"

"That's just the kind of scandal I can't use, Mr. Chambers."

"But your name's already in the papers."

"Simply that the police want to talk to Gordon Phelps. There's a difference between Gordon Phelps, an acquaintance of Vivian Frayne—and Gordon Phelps, Vivian's gentleman-friend-lover, if you know what I mean. Once I talked with them, they'd get that out of me, and that's just the kind of thing I don't want smeared over the papers. On the other hand, once this damned murder is solved—it's over. It's off the front pages. It's yesterday's news. I'd be out of it."

"Okay, okay," I said. "So just what did you do?"

23

"Sneaked out, called my lawyer, told him to come here, and sneaked back. As a matter of fact, that's the first time I've been out of this apartment in the last two days."

"Haven't been home?"

"No."

"What about your wife?"

"She's been down in Palm Beach for the last month."

"The lawyer get here?"

"Yes, and he was in quite a hurry, he had a plane to make for the West Coast. He stopped off, in a deuce of a hurry, on his way to the airport. Quickly, we worked out a thing. From the airport, he was to call the police. Supposedly, he had just seen the papers. He was to inform the police that I was out of town on business, and that I was due back in a couple of weeks. He was to tell them that he didn't know where I'd gone, just out of town on business, back in a couple of weeks. Then he was to send that telegram to Sierra. That would bring you in, and you'd be in charge."

"Kind of trust that Sophia Sierra, don't you?"

"In a cockeyed way, she's a friend. And her very avariciousness is on my side. Never hurts to do a favor for a rich man, does it?"

"All right," I said, "let's get down to cases. You knew this Vivian intimately for a few months. You say you're not involved in this killing. Did she have any special enemies, anybody she was especially afraid of—"

"Sophia Sierra," he said.

My head shot back as though a finger had been stuck in my eye. "Now how far can a man go when he's put out about not being able to make it with a dame—"

"That's not it, not at all." He was excited now and showing it. "I'm not accusing Sophia. You're asking. I'm telling. Vivian was afraid of her, she was convinced that Sophia was nursing a deep hatred. She mentioned it to me quite often—"

"Okay, okay, anyone else she mentioned?"

"No one else she mentioned."

"Anyone else she *didn't* mention?"

"Yes . . ." he said ruminatively, lifting a clenched hand and tapping a knuckle against his teeth. "Funny, this is the first time it's occurred to me . . . funny, it should have slipped my mind. . . ."

"What?" I said. "What?"

The hand went away from the mouth, clasped the other

hand, and he rocked as though he were praying. "Since I heard of this thing, I just haven't been able to think clearly. . . ."

"Are you thinking clearly now?"

"Yes, I think so."

"Okay, what's occurred to you?"

"A threat. A kind of threat."

"From whom? To whom?"

"From Steve Pedi to Vivian."

"Oh," I said, "so now we've got this Pedi back in again."

"A rough, tough, capable man," Gordon Phelps said. "I overheard a conversation, there at the Nirvana. . . ."

"When?"

"Oh, about a week ago. I was there, at the Nirvana. Vivian had gone upstairs—Pedi had his office upstairs. I had waited for her, at a table, and when she hadn't returned, I had gone up after her. Steve Pedi generally has one of his bouncers stationed outside his office, a big fellow, Amos Knafke, but at that moment Amos wasn't there. The door to Pedi's office was partly open and I was able to overhear the tail end of an argument between Vivian and Pedi."

"About what?" I said.

"I don't know."

"Well, what did you hear?"

"She was saying something like: '. . . and I'm just like a big sister to these kids. I know what's going on around here, and if it doesn't stop, I'll blow the whistle on the joint, so help me.' "

"And you have no idea what it was about?"

"None whatever."

"And you heard what Pedi answered?"

"It was something like: 'You and your frigged-up bluenose ideas. Butt out, or you'll get your head handed to you, and with a couple of holes in it.' "

I squinted at Gordon Phelps.

Gordon Phelps squinted at me.

"Interesting bit of dialogue," I said. "Then what happened?"

"I pushed in and they both greeted me with smiles, forced smiles, true enough, but smiles."

"Anyone else," I said, "on your list of possibilities—aside from yourself?"

"No one else," he said, "aside from myself."

I went away from him. I went to the window and looked out into the street. I said, with my back to him, "Where did she live, this Vivian Frayne?"

"115 East 64th."

"You visit her often?"

"I never visited her. Let's say . . . she visited here. Matter of fact, when I went off for vacations, she had carte blanche. She had a key to the place, of course."

"Of course." I turned to him. "When did she visit with you last, Mr. Phelps?"

He hesitated, but just for a moment.

"Last night," he said.

"She was murdered last night," I said, "wasn't she?"

"In her own apartment," he said, "not here."

"What time did she leave this apartment?"

"About midnight."

"Did you take her home?"

"No, she went home alone."

"Wasn't she working last night?"

"No, she had taken the night off."

"And had she continued about that hundred thousand dollar trip to Europe?"

"She had."

"And what did you tell her?"

"Told her I was still thinking about it."

"And when she left—what did you do?"

"I went to sleep. I was dead tired."

"Figures," I said, "you were dead tired."

"Why are you being sarcastic, Mr. Chambers?"

I had no answer to that question, so I ducked it. I took his hand and shook it. I said, "Good-bye, Mr. Phelps. You'll be right here, I take it?"

"At least until this thing blows over."

"Or blows up," I said.

"Chambers," he said, "you really think I did this, don't you?"

"I wouldn't know," I said.

"At the risk of being repetitious," he said, "I didn't."

"That's your story. We'll see how it holds up." I went to the door.

"Keep me informed," he said.

"I'll do my best."

"I want reports. Please."

"Which means I'll have to be coming back here."

"Naturally."

"Then we'll have to do it real whodunit, won't we?"

"I beg your pardon?" he said.

"You're not going to answer to everybody, are you—I mean like you answered to my ring today?"

"I saw you coming. I was watching at the window."

"You're not going to be spending all your time watching at the window, are you?"

"No," he said.

"Let's do a system, shall we? Let's make it five short rings, a pause, and then one long ring. Like that you'll know it's Prometheus bringing fire to man."

"Excellent, Mr. Prometheus. A very good idea, really. I hadn't thought of that at all."

There was a good deal, it appeared, that Mr. Gordon Phelps had not thought of.

SIX

He had not thought, for instance, of the possibility that a lady named Sophia Sierra might be attracted to a member of *homo sapiens*, gender male, without such member depositing a bag of loot at her feet like a sacrifice at an altar. He had not thought of the possibility that Sophia Sierra might be attracted to an individual half *his* age without such individual having to barter for her affections as though they were jewels for trade in a forbidden marketplace (I realized, quickly enough, that I was being utterly subjective and answering to the pique of my peculiar soul, and I realized that I was an employee, and, as such, I should shove being subjective and pandering to pique of soul, so I went on from there). Gordon Phelps had not thought, for instance, that he had absolutely no alibi: the fact that he said that he was alone in his hideaway apartment during the time of the murder of Vivian Frayne was exactly that—no alibi. He had not thought of the fact that he was a prime suspect, adorned, like a harpooned whale, by three deadly shafts, and all of them sticking out of him: motive, opportunity, proximity. He had not thought of the fact that, even if innocent, he was withholding information necessary and pertinent to police investigation of a capital crime. He had not thought of the fact that, no matter what his lawyer had told the police, they were, right now, in all probability, making every effort to seek him out and take him in. He had not thought of the fact that perhaps the police *had* thought of the fact that the lawyer was transporting a load of fertilizer shipped direct by the client. He had not thought of the fact that, perhaps, even Sophia Sierra——

I stopped it right there.

Once it was back to Sophia Sierra——I stopped it.

I flailed fingers at a cab and we had a glue-like ride through the morass of New York traffic to the precinct station wherein were housed the minions of the law devoted to Homicide in that section of Manhattan. There, too, was housed the brain and bulk of one Detective-Lieutenant Louis Parker, staunchest of the minions of the law: cop, friend, gentleman, human being. And there I was informed, after prodding lesser minions, that Parker was not due back in his office until eleven o'clock in the evening. So I went to the bank to deposit five thousand dollars, but it was after three and the bank was closed, and since my office is equipped with an office-safe, I went to the office.

My secretary, Miss Miranda Foxworth, ancient, creaking, forthright, lovable, and ever-complaining of her psychosomatic arthritis, was bundled in her coat and reaching for the door when I entered.

"Hi," she said. "I was just going home."

"Bon voyage," I said. "Any messages?"

"Nothing," she said, a glint in her shrewd eyes. "But I sent you a message, in person, and what a message! What are you doing here? You slipping?"

I showed her the money. "Bank's closed," I said, "so I'm using the safe."

"That dame came bearing money? I don't believe it."

"The money's from a man."

"But I sent a gal."

"And she sent me to a man."

"And you went? You *are* slipping." She patted my cheek. "Anything you want?"

"Nothing, thanks. Go home."

"I'm going," she said and she went.

I put the money into the safe, absently twirled the dial, absently lit a cigarette, absently went into the inner office, sat down at my desk, put my feet up, closed my eyes, and played free-association with myself. The first thing my mind flushed was Nirvana. I was just reaching into Nirvana when the raucous peal of the phone pulled me back. I lifted the thing.

"Hello?" I growled.

"Mr. Peter Chambers?" It was a lady's voice spacing each syllable in precise enunciation. The question was practically a pronunciamiento.

"This is he," I said, carefully grammatical.

"Barbara Phelps, here," she said.

"Beg pardon?" I said, but my feet came off the desk.

"Mrs. Gordon Phelps," she said. "This *is* Mr. Chambers, isn't it?"

"Yes, yes, Chambers," I said.

"I should like to see you, if you please, Mr. Chambers? Are you available?"

"Yes, Mrs. Phelps, I'm available."

"Could you come here?"

"Where?" I said.

"My home. 2225 Fifth Avenue."

"When?" I said.

"Right now, if you please, Mr. Chambers. Can you make it?"

"Yes, ma'am, I can make it."

"Very good," she said and she hung up and there I was, sitting somewhat on the edge of my seat, holding a receiver in my hand and shaking my head to relieve my mind of the persistent poking of free-association Nirvana.

SEVEN

A butler opened the door for me, a real-life, motion-picture-type, British-accented, butler. In uniform. "Who, please?" he uttered.

"Chambers," I uttered right back at him.

"Oh this way please," said he. "The drawing room."

The drawing room was a gorgeous cavern with stained-glass windows that did iridescent tricks with the dying sun of the early evening. There were two denizens within the gorgeous cavern, both of whom stood up, as the butler discreetly withdrew after discreetly announcing: "Mr. Chambers, Madame."

There was a lady and a gentleman, except the gentleman was no gentleman. His name was Adam Frick and he and I had had business together but a private richard learns to be almost as discreet as a British-accent butler, so I did not recognize him. He was tall, lithe, lean and young, with blond hair and blue eyes, and he was death-on-wheels to susceptible damosels, and if they were not susceptible, he made them susceptible.

I had never seen the lady before.

"I'm Mrs. Phelps," she said, "Barbara Phelps. This is Adam Frick. Mr. Frick is the pilot of our private plane. Mr. Frick, Mr. Chambers."

"I know Mr. Chambers," Frick said. He said it first.

"Of course," I said. "How are you, Mr. Frick?"

"Very well, thank you," he said. He was holding a snifter glass of brandy in his right hand. He shifted it to his left hand, extended his right hand, and we shook. The hand had all the warmth of the fin of a fish. He moved off, a graceful figure in sport jacket and tweed slacks. He was a most competent pilot who had been fired from a national airline because he had raped an airline hostess. The hostess had not been entirely innocent. She had been enamored of his baby-blue eyes, his wavy blond hair, his slick manners, and his concave-belly charm. She had led him on but she had not realized she was dealing with a gentleman who had a conscience vaguely equivalent to the conscience of a hyena. She had been a virgin begging to be raped, and Adam Frick did not have to be begged, but the young lady had had religious scruples against such type of intrusion, and she had screamed. It had developed into the usual mess, which was when Adam Frick had become my client. I had uncovered twelve airmen who had gone to bed with the young lady, doing aeronautical maneuvers whilst keeping the hymen intact, and such disclosures had a mitigating effect upon the screaming young lady. She had refused to sign an official complaint, and the

matter was dropped. So was Adam Frick, but he had retained
his license, and now he turns up as Mrs. Barbara Phelps' private pilot, which made Mrs. Barbara Phelps a very interesting
lady, indeed.

"Would you like a drink, Mr. Chambers?" she said.
"Brandy?"

"No, thank you," I said. "I don't drink."

Adam Frick's eyebrows almost hit his hairline, but he said
nothing. Everybody was being discreet today.

"Adam," she said, "I'd like a bit more brandy, please."

"Yes, of course," he said.

"Please sit down, Mr. Chambers," Barbara Phelps said.

She was on the pale side of forty, top-heavy with slim hips
and breasts that stuck out like cannons from a bastion. She
had good legs, age-revealing lines on her neck, and dark-
brown, eager, passionate eyes. The way she looked at Adam
Frick, that young man was earning his pay as private pilot.

"I'm worried about my husband," she said.

"Yes ma'am," I said. "I'll do my best."

Adam brought her the drink. She sipped before she spoke.
"We've been at Palm Beach," she said.

"Yes ma'am," I said.

"Returned two days ago," she said.

"Yes ma'am," I said.

"Gordon was not about, but that's not unusual. Frankly,
I hardly thought about it." She sipped. "Have you seen the
papers, Mr. Chambers?"

"Yes ma'am," I said.

"I called Gordon's office. They haven't heard from him in
two days. I don't generally worry about Gordon but I am
worried now."

"I understand, ma'am," I said.

"Gordon has great confidence in you, Mr. Chambers."

"Thank you, ma'am," I said.

"I want you to find him for me."

"Yes ma'am," I said. "I'll do my best."

She put her glass aside. She touched a hand to her blue-
gray hair. Blue-gray hair gave distinguished frosting to the
passionate eyes. She frowned, observing me sidelong. The
"yes ma'ams" were getting to her. She arose, strode briskly
to a desk, drew a checkbook and wrote a check. "Here," she
said imperiously.

The check was for a thousand bucks.

"Thank you, ma'am," I said. "I'll do my best."

"Find him for me. Just tell him to call me so that I know he's all right."

"Yes ma'am," I said.

"The papers are crazy," she said. "Gordon might play around with a tramp like that. But he wouldn't take her seriously enough to kill her." But now she was not looking at me, she was looking at Adam Frick.

I did not ask her how she knew the lady was a tramp.

She looked back to me. "Thank you very much," she said. I was dismissed. Her Majesty had dismissed me.

"Yes ma'am," I said.

Adam Frick took me to the door.

"I want to talk to you," he said.

"Talk," I said.

"Not here. Not now."

"How come she called me?" I said. "How come she didn't call her own boy?"

"Her own boy?"

"Si Murray."

"How do you know?" he said.

"I know everything," I said.

He looked at me almost admiringly. "She figures you're close to Phelps, figures you might have a line on him."

"I might," I said.

"I want to talk to you. Please."

"About this?"

"Yes."

"All right. When?"

He glanced over his shoulder. There was no one behind him. "I'll be stuck in this damned prison for a while. Call me late tonight. You know where I live. You still have the phone number?"

"Yes."

"If I'm not there, I'll be there. But call me. Please."

"I'll call you, kid."

"Thanks," he said.

He opened the door for me. I stepped out into the carbon monoxide of Fifth Avenue. I breathed deeply of the foul city air. It was resuscitating.

EIGHT

I went to a restaurant and ordered a leisurely dinner which I consumed with a bright appetite and a blank mind. I went home, shook free from my clothes, and napped, the alarm clock in my head set for nine o'clock. I did not dream. At nine o'clock I sat myself into a warm tub and turned on the thinking, such as it was. I thought about Gordon Phelps (having his own kind of fun as George Phillips), and Barbara Phelps (having her own kind of fun as Barbara Phelps), and Vivian Frayne (whose fun had stopped suddenly), and Sophia Sierra (and Phelps' admonishment that she was as mercenary as an ancient Hessian), and Adam Frick (whose voice had been tinged with fright when he had pleaded to talk to me), and Steve Pedi (who owned a dance hall), and the Nirvana Ballroom (which was the dance hall Steve Pedi owned).

Nirvana Ballroom. I was back to free-association.

Nirvana, an expression contained in Buddhism. Buddhism, a philosophy and religion in strong existence in the sixth and fifth centuries before Christ. Buddhism, which taught that pain and suffering were an integral part of life, and that release could only be obtained through self-denial, guiltlessness, rejection of the passions, and concentration upon the exclusion of all things of the senses. Utter release, at final, is Nirvana: the epitome of selflessness, the actuality of blissful nonexistence. In Buddhist theology, the extinction of individual existence, the extinction of pain and suffering, the extinction of all desire and passion—is the entrance into Nirvana: the attainment of perfect beatitude. I thought, as I climbed out of my warm tub, that to some of us Nirvana can signify the beginning to true life, but to others, Nirvana can also mean death.

NINE

At ten o'clock in the evening—fresh, clean, unsullied, and unphilosophical—I presented myself at the Nirvana Ballroom. It was on Broadway at Fifty-fifth beneath a neat marquee which declared simply: NIRVANA. I paid an admission fee of one dollar and fifty cents, trudged up a flight of stairs, passed through an archway, and entered upon a crowded blue dimness. The large parallelogram of smooth-floored dance hall held more suckers than a spiritualists' convention competing for séances at cut-rate prices. There were at last a hundred couples on the floor swaying in various embraces to swoosh-soft music wafted from an excellent orchestra on a podium to the right. Each close-pressed couple seemed oblivious of any of the other close-pressed couples, and oblivious they well might be in the almost-dark of slowly revolving chandeliers spraying pin-point beams of pale blue light. I had to squint to get accustomed to the gloom of the manufactured lovers' twilight. To my left, there was a carpeted stairway, going up. In front of me was a wooden barrier with swinging-gate entrances to the dance-floor proper. Shapely young ladies in enticing attitudes lounged against the inner section of the barrier. They smiled invitingly at each new customer as he entered and the customer either smiled in return or gaped in embarrassment: the ladies were encased in shimmering evening gowns that sheathed their bodies more clingingly than Bikinis. I moved along the barrier seeking Sophia and could not find her. I found a velvet roped-off section, in an area even dimmer than the rest of the place, which contained chairs and tables and huddled couples. I also found a bar.

I went to the bar.

"Scotch and water," I said.

"Sorry, no hard stuff," the bartender said.

"A bottle of beer," I said.

"Sorry, no beer," the bartender said.

"This a bar?" I said.

"It's a bar," the bartender said, "but we don't serve no beverages what's got alcohol. It ain't allowed by law. We got coffee, raisin cake, all kinds soft drinks, soda, and ice cubes if you need them. This the first time you been here, Mac?"

"First time," I said. "Got a date with a young lady, kind of."

"Gal working here?"

"Yeah, but I can't seem to find her."

The bartender grinned sympathetically. "It's a little dark when you first come in, but when you're dancing with one of them chicks, believe me you appreciate it like that—dark. If you tell me what chick you're looking for, maybe I can help."

"Sophia Sierra."

"Sophia? Man, you got taste. Man, that's a chick what's got everything, and got it all in the right places." He jerked his head toward the roped-off area. "She's sitting there with some broken-down joe. He ain't nothing, Mac. My money's on you."

"Thanks," I said and started for the chairs and tables.

"Hey," the bartender called.

I went back to the bar. If his call was a hint for a tip, he was entitled to it. I reached for my wallet but he stopped me.

"Nah," he said, "it ain't that. It's only you ain't allowed in there without no tickets." Now he jerked his head toward a booth that was fitted out like a box-office for a movie house. "Over there," he said. "They're a buck for ten tickets, each ticket a dance, but a dance is prackilly thirty seconds. Got a tip for you, Mac, seeing as you're new here. Got two tips. Get a whole load of tickets if you want to make a hit with any of them gals, especially Sophia, she's class. And tip two, don't tangle with none of them bouncers. You'll see them on the floor. They're single-o, they cruise around, and they're on the bruiser-type, but big, big. Not that they'll bother you none, except you really start climbing all over a broad and maybe sticking your hand down her dress, though a classy-looking feller like you, you don't figure. . . ."

"Thanks again," I said and this time I dipped into the

wallet and handed over a bill and this time he did not refuse me.

"Thank you," he said, "and remember about that load of tickets, Mac. I'm with you."

At the booth, I offered twenty dollars.

"Tickets," I said to a protuberant redhead who was resting on her bosom.

"How many?" she said, squirting a small smile.

"The works," I said, with bravado.

"Yes, sir," she said and the smile widened to a display of bad bridgework. "Yes sir, sport. Here you go."

She peeled off an impressive batch of tickets and I held them aloft like a torch as I maneuvered through the dimness seeking Sophia.

I found her.

Off in a corner, she was seated at a table vis-à-vis to a grizzled little man whose wizened face surrounded a pair of glittering eyes that could have hypnotized a snake. I hated to break up the party, but after all, I had a date. I touched her shoulder and she looked up. He looked up too, and the beady little eyes were so suffused with elderly torment that I began shooting off my mouth like I was munching firecrackers.

"Sorry," I said. "Just flew in from Las Vegas to see my girl. It's kind of a one-night stand, just tonight. Got to be back on the job tomorrow. Got to make a living, you know. Hate to cut in like this. But we're engaged, you know. Tough, when you're in Vegas and you've got a girl in New York. I do hope you understand, Mr. . . . Mr. . . ."

"Feninton," he piped. "Hiram Feninton."

"Oh, I told you he'd come," Sophia said. "I told you I was hoping he'd make it, Mr. Feninton."

"Yes, yes, you did," Mr. Feninton said. He stood up, a small bow-legged man. "Youth, youth," he said. "I envy you your youth, young man." His hand fumbled in his pocket, brought out a sheaf of bills, and he peered intently as he selected one and handed it to me. (Subtlety, it appeared, was foreign to Nirvana.) "Here," he said. "Please take it. Let Feninton play Cupid to young love tonight." He looked down at Sophia. "Don't let him spend any money tonight. Let it be on me, on me." Then his other hand reached into another pocket and he slipped me a pint bottle that had the feel of a whiskey bottle. "On me, on me," he said. "Let this

evening be on me." He bowed toward her, his glittering eyes
consuming her. "We'll make it another evening, Miss Sophia."
He smiled at me. "An old man, a harmless old man. Well,
good-bye now." And he turned abruptly and his bowlegs
carried him away into the dimness.

I sat down, still holding the money and still holding the
bottle. Almost at once my knees met her knees beneath the
table, and almost at once one of mine was taken by two of
hers, like a caress, and held warmly.

"I'm so darn glad you came," she said.

On top of the table, there was a tray which held a small
bucket of ice cubes, four glasses, six swizzle sticks, and a
bottle of seltzer. In front of her, the amber contents of a
glass was down near the bottom. In front of me, a glass
was empty except for one melting ice cube.

"I'm a little bit drunkie," she said, the pressure of her
knees tightening. "Got a little drunkie, waiting for you,
hoping you'd show up."

"I thought the hard stuff wasn't allowed here," I said.

"It's not. Dance halls don't have a license for liquor in this
town. But you can kind of bring it in yourself, and they
supply you with set-ups."

"And Mr. Feninton brought it in?"

"He sent out for it." She took her glass and my glass
and set them on the tray. She took two clean glasses and
put one in front of me and one in front of her. "What's
left in the bottle?" she said.

There was not much. I emptied it, half in her glass, half
in mine. It was Scotch, of an expensive brand. "A real sport,
Mr. Feninton," I said.

"We don't get them too often here, believe me."

"What do I do with the empty bottle?"

"Just put it on the floor under the table."

I did that and her hand suddenly caught mine beneath the
table. I looked across at her. Her smile was warm, soft, de-
mure, but the expression about her eyes was peculiar. Somehow, it looked like contempt.

Her hand released mine and she took up the seltzer bottle,
holding it poised over my glass. "How much do you like?"
she said.

"Up to half, please."

"Me too," she said and squirted seltzer into my glass
and into hers. She put the bottle back on the tray, stirred

her drink, stirred mine, laid away the swizzle stick and lifted her glass. "To us," she said. "To us, over and over again. I'm glad I met you. Really, I am."

"Over and over again," I said and we drank Mr. Feninton's whiskey. Then I brought up the bill the man had given me. "Have a donation," I said, "from Mr. Feninton. For young love out of Las Vegas."

"Hold it for me," she said, "I have no place to put it." She sighed. "Crumb joint, isn't it? Once in a while you get them like Feninton, but mostly they're crumbs."

"Sweetie," I said, "what the hell are you doing here?"

"Working," she said defiantly. "Let's put it this way—I'm working while I'm marking time. Where else can a girl earn maybe three hundred dollars a week? I mean, working honest?"

"This is honest?" I said.

"You're cute," she said.

"The hell with that," I said.

"Like my dress?" she said. "I wore it especially for you."

"What dress?" I said.

I did not see a dress. I saw white round arms, full white shoulders, the swell of smooth white breasts almost entirely exposed, and the top rim of a red silk evening gown, without front, without back, without sides.

"Who can see the dress?" I said.

"Would you like to see the dress?"

"I would love to see the dress."

"Would you like to dance? Like that you can see the dress. It's wild."

"I would like to do whatever you would like to do."

"I would like to dance," she said.

"Sold," I said. "Let's dance."

She stood up, and I just sat there, numbly clutching the dance tickets, as I stared up at her, feeling my mouth open as though pressure were being applied to my chin.

She was something. It was incredible.

It was nakedness: red nakedness: sheer red glistening nakedness: and yet it had a guileless magic that kept it from being obscene. It was a sheath of red silk, starting as an encirclement deep below the smooth caverns of her armpits and descending to an encirclement midpoint at the turn of her calves; it clung like a leotard, tight, bright, red silk membrane that produced the bold relief of a red silk body: red thigh, groin, loin, navel, bosom; rise and fall of red silk nakedness exploding to pinpoints of iridescence under the revolving blue of the chandeliers—it was something incredible. It set your heart to pumping in a passion like fright: thick black hair and wide black eyes, cream-white flesh, and the red-hugging, clinging nakedness of the dress. And yet it was not obscene: it was overwhelmingly, breath-takingly beautiful. That was it: a red silk dress, no stockings, and red silk spike-heeled shoes. She wore absolutely nothing else.

"Let's dance," she said.

I handed up the string of tickets.

"Forget that," she said and she flung the tickets to the table. "Let's do it like Mr. Feninton said. Let's make this evening on him."

That gave me a little moment of triumph. I stood up, thinking of Gordon Phelps. This was the girl who, according to him, had a steel-trap mind cast in the mold of a cash register. Maybe. Maybe, according to him. Maybe, as it applied to him. Maybe, as it applied to some others, many others, all others. But maybe does not encompass always, and if it does, maybe this was her time for not-always. Why not? Why cannot a girl flip for a guy, bing, like that, out of left field? And why cannot that guy be I? Why not? The hell with modesty. Why cannot a girl like Sophia Sierra go overboard, for some cockeyed reason of her own, for a man like Peter Chambers? Why not? Reverse it. Peter Chambers, for some cockeyed reason of *his* own, had gone overboard for Sophia Sierra. Bing. Like that. Out of left field. Why not?

I took her arm and led her to the blue-streaked dimness of the dance floor. We danced, but it was like kids around a Maypole. I mean I held her, but I kept my distance. So she laid her cheek to mine.

"Why don't you dance like everybody else?" she said at my ear. "You bashful, lover?"

I moved my head away and looked past her shoulder. Most of the swaying couples were more tightly pressed than an ancient rose in a lover's album.

"Like that," I said, "I'm bashful."

"Don't be," she said and her body moved to mine in a practiced rhythm, and her warm body yielded to mine, and we ground together, lightly, in a primitive embrace, swaying to the music. I did not gasp because I was ashamed to gasp.

And now her cheek was against mine again and her giggle was alive at my ear. "Perpendicular prostitution," she said. "It's part of the racket, taxi-dance racket. Who're the customers? Wackie-boys, nutty-boys, sex-bombs, scared-guys, crazos. Mostly, they're the customers—who else? Crazos looking for a crazy thrill. Okay, they buy enough tickets, we give them their crazy thrill. The faster we get rid of them, the faster we grab the next customer with a fistful of tickets. We get half the amount of the tickets they buy. That's the racket. The hell with it. What have we got to lose? Nothing, except once in a while we get a gown spoiled. Lousy racket, huh? But a gal has got to make a living, hasn't she? And at least it's legit. Why, take these gals working in the offices, these Gal Fridays, working for a fast fifty bucks a week, and making it with the boss on the side, and picking up a little extra spending money like that—"

"Let's go sit," I said.

"At least this is legit," she said. "Nobody's making it with anybody, the whole bit is strictly impersonal—"

"Let's sit," I said.

"You angry with me?"

"I'm nuts about you."

"That's the way I want it."

"Let's go sit."

"Whatever you say. You're the boss, lover."

"Let's sit," I said.

"Sure," she said, and she moved from me, and we danced for a few moments, as conservative as the minuet, and then we broke it up and hustled back to the table and sipped Feninton's highballs in silence, and then I said, "I saw G. Phillips."

"About time you opened up," she said. "I've been waiting."

"Why didn't you ask?"

"It's none of my business, though I've been dying."

"Of what?"

"Curiosity."

"You know what he wants?" I said.

"My guess—he wants to get out from under."

"You think he's mixed up in it?"

"My guess—yes. I wouldn't say this to the cops. I'm saying it to you."

"You think he killed her?"

"That's my hunch."

"Why?" I said. "Why should G. Phillips kill V. Frayne?"

"It's my hunch she was pushing him."

"How?"

"Sticking a finger in his ear. For a little blackmail."

I leaned back and I looked at her. She was a smart girl. A very smart girl. Too smart, perhaps.

"What kind of blackmail?" I said.

"I'm not quite sure. But when a guy's operating under a name that's not his own—he's open for it."

"Frayne knew that G. Phillips was Gordon Phelps?"

"Sure she knew. That's why she hooked him from me."

"Who told her?"

"Search me. But that guy was set up like a pin in a bowling alley. Leave it to V. Frayne to roll the ball."

"What about S. Sierra?"

"Now what the hell does that mean, lover?" She moved her glass aside, put her elbows on the table, clasped her hands, leaned her chin on her knuckles and stared at me.

"Means," I said, "that if he was a set-up for V. Frayne, he was just as much a set-up for S. Sierra. Logical?"

"No."

"Why not, pray?"

"Because, pray, there are people and people."

"Aren't there, for sure," I said.

"There are people who are capable of blackmail, and there are people who are not."

"And Sophia Sierra is not?" I suggested.

"You bet your ass she's not." Her Cuban temper loaded her eyes with fire. Her hand came across to my arm and I could feel the fingernails through my sleeve. Just for a fleeting irrelevant moment I thought about being in bed with her. "Oh, I'm no angel," she said, "don't think I'm trying to give you that idea. But there are people and people, and people are . . . complex, crazy, mixed-up. There are people who can kill but cannot steal. There are people who can steal but cannot kill. There are soft-hearted murderers and hard-hearted evangelists. There are people who can stick up a bank but they can't blackmail a sucker. There are extortionists that go to church every Sunday and really believe in God. There are thieves who give most of their loot to charity, and there are charity workers who are truly thieves. There are blackmailers who think that pickpockets are criminals, and there are pickpockets who think that blackmailers stink to high heaven. People have all kinds of quirks about what's right and wrong——"

"Okay," I said. "There are people and people. What kind of people are you?"

"I'm a people that thinks that blackmail is dirty and filthy and rotten. Now don't get me wrong. I can work a bunco game, I can take a sucker for a ride like he's on a toboggan, but I think that out-and-out blackmail is dirty and filthy and rotten——I could never go through with it. I couldn't do blackmail if my life depended on it."

"Could Vivian Frayne?"

"Sure-pop. Vivian was different people. She thought blackmail was smart, worked it pretty good in her lifetime."

"No kind word for the dead?" I said.

"Oh, there was another side to Vivian Frayne, I'll admit that. She could be good, kind, sweet——she was like a mother to most of the kids working in this joint, really like a mother, lent them money, worried over their problems, even gave them advice on their morals. That's what I mean about people, lover, nobody yet has made a straight pattern for people. Now Vivian——"

"You didn't particularly like her, did you?"

"That G. Phillips briefed you pretty good, didn't he?"

"All the way," I said.

"Well, I hated that bitch."

"Enough to kill her?"

"I admit I've got a temper."

"Temper enough to kill?"

"Only when it's at tip-top point."

"At what point was it with Vivian?"

"It had cooled down to a simmer." She smiled but her eyes remained serious. "You're a nosey son of a bitch, aren't you?"

"I'm being paid to be nosey."

"Like how much?" she said.

"Like five thousand dollars," I said.

Her posture eased. The smile grew broader. The eyes squinted. "At least that's a respectable buck," she said, "for being nosey." Now she threw me a mellow bordello glance. "Guys like you make lots of money, don't they?"

"Enough," I said, "for a fringe-type character. But fringe-type characters like Steve Pedi, I imagine, make more."

"Ah-ha," she said. "Now we're up to Steve Pedi."

"He threw you Phelps, didn't he?"

"Let's say he recommended him."

"But as Gordon Phelps, not as an anonymous G. Phillips."

"Yes, that's right."

"But Vivian had her hooks in right after you?"

"Yes, that's right."

"Upon Pedi's recommendation too?"

"That's a hundred percent wrong."

"All right," I said, "let's just stay on that for a moment, please. Pedi steered you to Phelps—as Phelps. Then Vivian moved in—because, according to Phelps himself, she knew who he was. Both you and Phelps seem certain that it wasn't Pedi who gave her the tip-off. Now, why, please, so certain?"

"Because Pedi wouldn't be doing favors for Vivian. That's simple enough, isn't it?"

"Why not?"

"Look," she said. "Vivian was an old-timer here. She was a very beautiful girl, she knew her way around, the customers loved her. But if she would have quit the joint, Steve wouldn't have been too unhappy."

"So why didn't he fire her?"

"I just don't think he had the nerve. She knew a lot of the ins-and-outs, she'd been here a hell of a long time. A girl like that can gossip. Why should Steve Pedi make an enemy?"

"Why didn't he like her?"

"In a way, she was a pest. She stuck her nose into everything. If you can think of a shop-foreman in a dance hall— Vivian was the shop-foreman. Any girl had a beef, she'd go to Vivian, and Vivian would take it to the boss. A boss likes that like he likes a toothache. Even when there were no special beefs, Vivian took over with complaints to the boss. She was always on his neck. Maybe she thought she had that right, by seniority. In every business, you get one like that. A pain in the ass to the boss, but the boss just hasn't the nerve to fire them."

"I'd like to meet this boss."

"How do you know he'd like to meet you?"

"He'll meet me," I said. "What kind of a guy is he?"

"A guy."

"Nice?"

"Nice like hell."

Mildly I said, "Now that doesn't sound real nice."

"Who gave you the idea that Steve Pedi was a nice guy?"

"Nobody. I was just asking. Look, I'd like to go talk to him. Take me, huh?"

"You're liable to get bounced on your ear, lover."

"By whom?"

"By an ape named Amos Knafke. Guardian of the portals."

"I'll take my chances with Knafke."

"Think you're big enough?"

"If not, I'll cut him down to size."

"At the risk of sounding sadistic," she said, "this is a show I think I'm going to enjoy watching. I'll play wet-nurse."

"To whom?"

"To you."

"Be my guest," I said. "In fact, be my guide."

TEN

She led me to the carpeted stairway, the stragglers on the other side of the barrier eye-popping her like vultures glimpsing bait. She stalked through them, imperious, oblivious, and I followed. Heads turned, eyes glistened, tongues licked at dry lips. Even here, at the Nirvana, where the commodity was enticement for perpendicular performance, Sophia Sierra stood out amongst her shapely sisters, moving tall and disdainful, as heads turned and eyes glistened and tongues licked at dry lips. I followed her up the carpeted stairway, and along a carpeted hallway. At the door at the end stood a massive man like a languorous behemoth.

"That's Knafke," she whispered.

"I'm thrilled," I said.

"Yeah?" he grunted as we approached.

"Steve Pedi," I said.

"So?" he said.

He was an enormous man but he had the muscle-bound movements of most big men. A ponderous belly stood out like an idealist among politicians. He could be had, if you were quick, and that would be the point of attack, the belly: it was wide-open and vulnerable.

"So who wants to see Mr. Pedi?" he said in a voice that sounded like gravel being sifted in a deep drum. "And furthermore he's busy."

"Busy with whom?" I said.

"Busy with himself."

"Please tell him," I said.

"What?"

"That I'd like to see him."

"Who the hell are you?"

"Peter Chambers. Please tell him."

Eyes drowned in the fat of a face veered to Sophia.

"Who's your boyfriend, Sophie?" he said.

"He wants to see Mr. Pedi," she said.

"About what?" he said.

"He wants to talk to him," she said.

The eyes came back to me. "If it's a complaint, buster, we got a complaint department. Mr. Pedi don't like no bother with the chumps."

"Amos," I said, "kindly go in and tell Mr. Pedi a chump would like to talk to him. And kindly, Amos, shake up that fat ass of yours."

"That's not nice language in front of a lady," he said gleefully. "And how do you know I'm Amos?"

"A birdie whispered to me. A pigeon."

"Oh, a wise weenie," he said with pleasure. "How come I always get them?" A large paw reached for my neck and his smile was almost slobbering in anticipation.

I hated myself for doing it.

He got two quick fists to the belly and they went in deep. He grunted but he bent, resistantly, like strong flame in wind. A knee to the groin bent him further and then a judo-shot to the nape of the neck flattened him to the floor, comatose and breathing stentoriously. I was ashamed as I stepped over him and opened Pedi's door.

"After you," I said.

Her eyes were wild. "Wow, you're crazy, you're a crazy man."

I hated her too, but I hated myself more.

She went through the open door and I followed her and closed it behind me. A handsome, white-faced man stood up behind a desk.

"Yes?" he said. "What is it? Hello, Sophia."

"Hello," she said and fell into a soft chair as though she were exhausted.

"Yes, what is it, please?" he said.

I looked about. It was a large room, its walls cluttered with autographed copies of photographs of celebrities. The furniture was tasteful, expensive and comfortable.

"He wants to talk to you," Sophia said.

"Where's Knafke?" he said and he frowned.

He was tall and lean. His clothes were tailor-made, narrow-lapeled and high-gorged. He was slim and elegant, with hollow cheeks, a patrician nose, and black, intelligent eyes, slanted and foreign-looking in the white face.

"Knafke is outside," Sophia said.

"Outside!" he said.

"This is Peter Chambers," Sophia said. "Mr. Chambers— Mr. Steve Pedi."

"How do you do?" I said.

"Knafke?" he said, blinking uncomprehendingly. "Outside?"

"I laid him out," I said.

He squinted at me. A hand went up to his hair, black hair, perfectly in place, tight against the sides, with a widow's peak in front. "You did what? You laid out who?" he said.

"Knafke," I said, "if that's the name of the gorilla who's supposed to play Horatius to your bridge." I do not like to admit it, but I was still impressing Sophia.

Pedi's mouth pulled thin against his teeth. He threw a glance at Sophia, another at me, came out from behind the desk, went to the door, opened it, cast a glance beyond, closed the door. He smiled with fine white teeth, every one of which was capped. He spoke to Sophia. "Who did you say this man was?"

"I didn't say who. All I said was his name."

"What's his name?"

"Peter Chambers."

He came to me. He extended his hand and I took it. For a slender man he had a lot of strength in his hand. "I'm glad to know you," he said. The capped teeth flashed brilliantly in a wider smile. "You wouldn't want Knafke's job, would you? Because if you would, you're hired. Right now."

"I'm not available," I said.

"Too bad," he said. "All right. What is it, please?"

The door opened. Knafke lumbered in.

"Where is he?" Knafke said. "Where is that mother-grabbing son of a bitch."

"I'm here," I said, softly.

"Get out of here, Amos," Pedi said. "Out, please." And as Knafke stood indecisively, Pedi repeated, "Out, out. Go watch the door."

Knafke looked at me, looked at Sophia, looked at his boss. Then his mouth twisted into a rueful fang-toothed smile. "Check," he said to me, "only I wish you should try this some other time, buster. I would like you should try this again."

"Any time," I said.

"I wish," Knafke said.

"Out, out," Pedi said. "Go watch the door."

"I only wish," Knafke murmured, as he left, quietly closing the door.

"All right, Mr. Chambers," Pedi said. "What's the beef?"

"It's personal, I think," I said.

"You mean you don't want Sophia?" Pedi said.

"It's up to you," I said. "It's personal as far as you're concerned, not me."

"Personal, like what?" he said.

"Personal like Vivian Frayne," I said.

"You heard the man, Soph," he said. "Will you wait for him downstairs, please." His smile had very little mirth as he added: "Where'd you find him?"

"I came to bring him a message," she said.

"Message," he said in bewilderment.

"She brought me a message," I said.

"Razzle-dazzle talk," he said irritably. "Ring-around-the-rosy. Okay, that's the way you want it, that's the way you got it, it's none of my business. Go wait for your friend downstairs, Soph. Please."

She rose, smiled at him, smiled at me, said, "See you," and moved to the door.

"Man, that's a dress," Steve Pedi said.

"Thank you," she said over her shoulder and went out.

He lit a cigarette, inhaled deeply, flicked the match to an ashtray. He lounged against the edge of the desk, one knee moving impatiently.

"All right," he said, "let's have it. What's this all about?" He had a smooth, controlled voice—which suited him. That was the sum of him, smooth, controlled—fighting for the smoothness and control—the ulcer type.

"Vivian Frayne," I said.

"You a cop?"

"No."

"The cops have been here."

"Of course," I said. "The gal worked here."

"What's your interest, pal?"

"I'm checking. I'm being paid to check."

"By whom?"

"It's not allowed that you talk when you're being paid to check. Wouldn't be fair potsy."

His voice suddenly had a bite like mustard. "All right, what do you want, Mac?"

"I want to know if you threatened Vivian Frayne."

He turned his back on me. He scratched out the cigarette in an ashtray. When he turned back, a meditative frown sat on his face. "Mac," he said seriously, "I got a few more around here like Amos. If I push a few buttons, I could have you chopped up like hamburger and thrown out on the seat of your ass."

"Why should you push buttons, Mac?"

"You know my name."

"And you know mine, Mac. So why should you want to push buttons?"

"Because you're poking around, and I don't like pokers. Now you want to play ball, okay, we play ball. If not, I'm starting to push buttons—Mac."

"What kind of ball, Stevie?"

"You want to level, Petie?"

"Sure," I said.

"Want to tell me who told you I threatened Vivian?"

"I might. There's no big top-secret mark on it."

"You a peeper?" he said. "Private?"

"It's time it got through to you, Stevie."

"Interested in a little extra dough?" he said.

"From whom?"

"From me."

"No," I said.

"You want to talk anyway?"

"Sure," I said.

"Okay. Who said I threatened Vivian?"

"George Phillips."

"That old son of a bitch! He's a liar."

"Want me to tell you what he told me?"

"I want," he said.

I told him.

"That old son of a bitch," he said when I was finished. "He's a liar."

"All right. Thanks. Just checking," I said and moved toward the door.

"Just a minute."

"Yes, Stevie?"

"The cops didn't mention none of this to me."

"So what do you want from me?" I said.

"You think they're playing it cool?"

"I wouldn't know."

"They pick up Gordon Phelps yet?"

"I don't know."

"You know who Phelps is?"

"Phillips," I said.

"You know plenty," he said, "don't you?"

"A little," I said.

"What I mean," he said. "If the cops picked him up, he must have spilled this crap to them too. What do you think?"

"If they did, he did, that's what I think."

He regarded me for a long moment. He smiled a remote thoughtful smile. He went to the desk, yanked a drawer, brought out three crisp one hundred dollar bills. "How you fixed for ethics?" he inquired.

"I'm fixed," I said.

"One answer to one question," he said, holding the money like a bouquet. "How about it, if it don't crash with the ethics?"

"Let's hear," I said.

"Did the cops pick up Phelps yet?"

"No," I said.

I took his three hundred dollars.

"Thanks," he said.

"It didn't crash with the ethics," I said.

"Look," he said, "will you kind of keep me informed on how the thing goes? I ain't mixed in this, but I got my flanks to protect, if you know what I mean."

"I know what you mean," I said.

"Will you keep me informed?"

"I might, if it doesn't crash with the ethics."

"Thanks," he said and he walked to the door with me and opened it. "This is Peter Chambers," he said to Amos Knafke. "He's a real nice fella. Any time he wants to see me, it's my pleasure."

"You're the boss, boss," Amos said.

"Good-bye, Mr. Chambers," Pedi said. "You're a real nice fella. I respect a guy with ethics. I like you very much."

"I'm thrilled," I said.

" 'Bye now," he said and closed the door and left me alone in the corridor with Amos.

"I'm sorry, Mr. Knafke," I said.

"For what?" he said.

"I'm a nothing," I said. "A wise weenie. I was making with the showboat. I was trying to impress the girl."

"Figures," he said. "Most of the finks here try to make it with a girl just like that. Only most of the finks here wind up with their nose in their mouth when they try to make it with a girl like that. You didn't. I would love for you to try again, but the boss says you're a nice fella, you're a nice fella. I only work here."

"I don't think this really evens it up, Mr. Knafke," I said, "but I hope it helps."

I stuffed Pedi's three hundred dollars into the meat of his palm.

ELEVEN

The lady in red was morosely stirring the dregs of Feninton's drink with the jagged end of a broken swizzle stick.

"How'd you make out?" she said.

"I laid a foundation," I said.

"Laid?" she said. "A foundation?"

"It's a term in my trade," I said.

"Sit down," she said. "Just don't stand there."

"I've got to go," I said.

"Are you crazy?" she said. "Go where?"

"I've got work to do."

"Wow, you're a miserable one, aren't you?"

"Better you found that out right at the beginning."

Her dark eyes came up. "I want you to stay."

"I'd love to, but I can't."

The eyes went back to the swizzle stick. "Will you come back?"

"I'll try."

"I want you to come back."

"I said I'll try."

"We're open here until four, you know."

"I'll try. I'll try my damndest."

"Try," she said. "Please. Please try."

TWELVE

A young cop kept me waiting outside of Parker's office for fifteen minutes but when I went in there was no one there but Parker. "Is this a new bit, Lieutenant?" I said. "Keeping the customers cooling their heels? Has the Lieutenant reached the point of half-ass tycoon, where the customer *must* wait outside otherwise the ego inside gets deflated?"

"Shut up," he said. "I was on the phones."

There were five phones on the desk, all of them quiet now. "I'm frigged on a case," Parker said, "and it's a bitcheroo because the corpse had a lot of glossy photos of herself, all of them sexy. So the newspapers won't lay off."

"Vivian Frayne?" I said.

"You read the wrong papers," he said. "There's no education in cheap tabloids." He sighed, stood up, rubbed a hand across his stiff black crew-cut. He was short, broad, thick and stocky, with a ruddy face and bright dark eyes. "What brings you?" he said. "I'm told you were here before."

"The cheap tabloids," I said.

He did not move. His eyes were amused. He grabbed at his mouth and held it as he studied me, his head nodding.

Then the hand fell away and he opened his arms and bowed like the burlesque of a corny prima donna reacting to applause. "Okay," he said, "I feel a cockeyed deal coming on. A Peter Chambers special. What do you know, and what must I do to find out what you know?"

"Don't have to do a thing," I said, "except tell me about Vivian Frayne."

"And for that . . . ?" he said.

"I might produce Gordon Phelps."

That rocked him. He jumped as though he'd been unexpectedly pinched in an unexpected place, but he righted himself quickly enough. He pursed his lips, cleared his throat, and glared at me like papa might glare at a favorite son who had stuffed his favorite pipe with toilet paper. "Oho," he said. "A *real* Peter Chambers special. I want that guy and I want him badly. You working for him?"

"I'm afraid I am."

"Can you produce him?"

"I can."

"Will you?"

"Depends."

"On what?"

"On how soon you want him."

"I want him right now."

"I can't produce him right now."

"When can you?"

"Let's talk it up a little, shall we, Lieutenant? You help me, I'll help you. It's the same old story: we're on the same side, you and I. It's only the approach that may be different."

"It may be, mayn't it?" he said but he was smiling.

"You're law and order. I'm law and disorder, I suppose. You're bound by Department rules. I have no rules, except the ones I make for myself."

"Law and disorder," he said and he chuckled. "I'll buy that." He went behind his desk, lay back in his swivel chair, lit up a cigar. "We're anxious on that Gordon Phelps. I'd like to squeeze that out of you."

"We're past the squeezing stage, you and I."

"Yeah." He growled behind cigar smoke. "Lawyer guy wafted us some cock and bull."

"I know about that," I said.

"Figured you would." He sat up. "When will you have him for me?"

"Let's say forty-eight hours. Maybe sooner, but let's say forty-eight hours at the outside. I'll either bring him in or I'll convince him to come in. Good enough?"

"And if we pick him up before that?"

"Then you pick him up," I said. "But one proviso, please. I don't want a tail on me. I'd lose him anyway, but why have to bother?" I did a grin for him, as boyish as I could muster it. "We got a deal, Lieutenant?"

"You got a deal, young fella."

Eagerly I said: "Gimme."

"Ain't much, really." He wrinkled his face, concentrating. "Dance-hall dame. Been in New York about thirteen years. Wise little operator, lived pretty good. Never in trouble. The gals in the dance hall adored her, she was kind of like a mother-hen to them. Investigation shows she'd been to Montreal and Hollywood a couple of times, and that's all we know about her."

"What about background?" I said.

"Nothing," he said, "which isn't unusual. Vivian Frayne's probably not her real name. Dame comes in from Oshkosh somewhere when she's about seventeen, probably a runaway, or a go-offer with a guy. Breaks family ties, gives herself a fancy name, gets lost in a city of nine million. Once there's no record on them—you just can't trace them back."

"What about those published pictures?"

"Those don't help either in these kind of cases. These are sophisticated glossies—who can tie up this gorgeous mature woman with the kid of seventeen that scrammed Oshkosh. Even if she has family, and they haven't forgotten all about her, those pictures wouldn't make the connection."

"No mail from any family?"

"Nothing."

"Okay, Lieutenant. Now let's have it."

"I'll do it chronologically."

"Yes, please, but do it, I'm real anxious to hear."

"Sequence started Monday night, late Monday night."

"Today's Wednesday," I said.

"She left the dance hall about four ayem Monday night, went home. After the cab dropped her, two guys approached, a mug job. One stuck a knife in her back, the other did the armlock bit around her throat. But as luck would have it, a cop turned the corner and saw the deal. They grabbed her bag and blew, but she struck out at one of them. She hit him and the knife dropped. The cop chased them, but they out-ran him. That's it for Monday night."

"Did she get a view of either one of them?" I said. "I mean to recognize?"

"No."

"Okay, I've got Monday night."

"It was a straight mugging, what with grabbing the bag, all in pattern. But we had the knife. There was one faint smudge of a print on it, and the lab boys did a hell of a job. Worked all of Tuesday, and finally came up with it. Turns out to be a grifter named Mousie Lawrence. Ever hear of Mousie Lawrence?"

"Vaguely," I said.

"A one-time loser, did a term about fifteen years ago for armed robbery, and that's the last we heard of him—until now. Fifteen years is a long time. New hoodlums grow up, you kind of lose track of the old ones, if they stay clean. Didn't even know this guy was in New York. Anyway, early this morning, about seven o'clock, cops come calling on Vivian Frayne with the gallery-photo of Lawrence."

"I thought you said she got no view of them."

"This was a different approach," he said. "Just wanted to ask if she'd ever seen the guy in the photo. After all, these guys were waiting for her practically at her apartment house. Maybe they did a case-job first at the dance hall, maybe they'd got acquainted with her. Wouldn't hurt to have her look at the photo. Reasonable?"

"Yes, sir," I said.

"There was no answer to their ring. One of the cops was a guy with brains, or maybe an impatient guy. He went down to the super and had him open the door. They found her inside, five bullets in her, a gun on the floor beside her. The apartment was upside down, it had been thoroughly searched. And mind you, when the super had opened the door, it had been locked—from the outside."

"Deadlock type of lock?"

"Yeah. You had to turn the knob on the inside to lock it, or lock it with a key from the outside. Whoever murdered her locked it from the outside. Anyway, that's when I got into this, personally. When they're dead, it's for Homicide."

"Think the mugging had anything to do with the murder?"

"Doesn't figure. Whoever killed her was able to get in and out of that apartment, that's for sure. If those babies were able to get in, that's where they would have been—if the job was for murder. But they were loitering outside, so they figure for muggers, not murderers. But we checked that angle anyway. Had Lawrence's photo passed around the dance hall, but the kids were clammed. Either they never saw the guy, or they're afraid to mix with a hood. Kids in dance halls are hip kids, they stay away from trouble, and it's trouble, let's face it, when you identify a hood."

"Got a photo for me?" I said.

"Sure. Had a lot of them made. We're looking for the guy." He opened the middle drawer of his desk and gave me two photographs, each about four by six. One was full face and one was profile. I looked at them briefly and put them away.

"Figure a time of death?" I said.

"About one o'clock Tuesday night."

"Wasn't she supposed to be working then?"

"Took the night off. Had a date."

"Any idea whom she had the date with?"

"She had a date with your client."

"Really," I said and I shifted the subject. "The place was thoroughly searched, you say. So whoever killed her was looking for something."

"Whatever they were looking for—they found."

"How would you know that, professor?"

"Because we did a pretty good search ourselves. We found nothing that meant anything to anybody. All we got was the gun right there on the floor, an insurance policy, and a diary."

"Without a diary, it wouldn't be a dame," I said.

"That diary gave us our first pinch."

That hit me right between the eyes. "You mean you've made an arrest in this case?"

"Arrested and released."

"Who?"

"A guy named Adam Frick."

"*Who?*"

"Adam Frick! What's the matter with you, you hard of hearing? An angle-bird who's a pilot. The diary gave us Frick. He was Frayne's light-of-love, plus her life insurance for twenty-five G's was in his favor, plus he has a key to the joint."

"And you released him?"

"We've got rules, remember?"

"You mean he had an alibi?"

"He said he was home sleeping. Lives over at the Wadsworth Arms. Said he'd tucked himself in at eleven o'clock."

"And you *released* him?"

"Look, any quack lawyer would have gotten him out. We got *habeas corpus* in this country. Just because a guy's got a policy in his favor, and he's got a key—that's no proof that he committed murder. Oh, he's still a suspect, but your Gordon Phelps is a much more likely candidate."

"What about the gun?"

"That was the murder weapon. Now look—stop squirming away from Phelps."

"All right," I said. "How'd he get into this?"

"Dear old diary," Parker said. "It gave us Adam Frick all spelled out. For the other guy we got only initials—G.P."

"This G.P. have a key to the place?"

"Diary specifically says no. Diary says G.P. was never even at the apartment. Though I bet she was at his. There's one key on her ring that we haven't found a door for. I bet G.P. is behind that door somewhere. She saw G.P. Tuesday night just before she came home to get killed."

"How do you know that, Lieutenant?"

"Diary states the date with G.P."

"Brother," I said, "you disappoint me." I went to the door. "In my book you used to be a guy who didn't figure to jump to conclusions."

"Who's jumping?"

"Why link initials G.P. to Gordon Phelps?"

"Believe me, I'm not jumping."

"Lieutenant," I said. "I'd like to see that apartment."

He looked dubious.

"You really want Phelps?" I said.

"Badly."

"Okay, I compromise. You can have him within twenty-four hours. Now can I see that apartment?"

Again he opened his desk drawer and dipped into it. He threw me a bunch of keys.

"You know the address?" he said.

"Yes," I said.

"Good luck," he said.

"Any prints on the gun?" I said.

"None," he said. "Smudges, no prints. And no prints in the apartment that could do us any good."

"It's still bothering me," I said.

"What?"

"Your *not* jumping to conclusions—about Phelps."

"No prints on the gun," he said.

"You told me."

"But there was a serial number on the gun."

"There generally is, unless it's filed off."

"This one wasn't filed off. It checked out. It belonged to a fellow with initials G.P. It belonged to a gentleman playboy by the name of Gordon Phelps."

THIRTEEN

I trudged the city streets from the precinct station house toward Broadway. I dangled keys in my pocket and facts in my brain. The keys jumbled and so did the facts. Parker knew nothing and neither did I. I had a couple of extra facts, but still I knew nothing. I knew where I could lay my hands on Gordon Phelps, and Parker didn't, but that did not bring me any closer to the same solution Parker was seeking. And I knew more about Mousie Lawrence than Parker did, but that was because Parker was law and order and I was law and disorder. The Police Department has its hands full. Crime in a big city is as multiple as the progeny of polygamy. Police minds cannot loiter in the past: they have enough to engage them in the present. Policemen have little time for casual gossip and there are not many who choose policemen to gossip with, especially if the subject matter of the gossip is criminal. Commit a crime that is public knowledge and you are immediately a special-interest target of the constituted authorities, but no matter how many crimes you commit, unless they have pierced the public knowledge, you attract about as much attention as a philanderer in theatrical circles. Professional criminals lust after inattention. Anonymity is a prize, facelessness an attribute, nonentity a requisite for continuing success—and yet, criminal activity, of necessity, must cross with the culture, there must be dealings with other beings, there must be a widening crisscross of intercourse, which in sum total is a part of knowledge, though a very private knowledge. The peeper has more ready access to this nether world of knowledge than the cop. A peeper is private. A cop is public. If a peeper is trusted, a private world is open to him that would amaze the public cop. Or maybe it would not amaze the public cop, if the public cop were a thoughtful man.

I knew more about Mousie Lawrence than Parker did.

Mousie Lawrence, born Morris Lawrence, was a fifty-year-old man with all the moral scuples of a despondent rodent. He was small, wiry, rough, tough and heartless. Fifteen years ago he was still groping, clawing for his niche in the world of his peers—that was when he was apprehended and jugged for armed robbery. But Mousie was not stupid and he had come a long way since then. Ten years ago, he had hooked up with a major narcotics outfit operating out of Mexico City, and he had been paired off with Kiddy Malone. They had fitted together like a screw and bolt, they had complemented one another: they were a rousing success in the nefarious traffic which was their milieu. They were front men, advance men, salesmen. Operating out of Mexico City, with enormous funds at their disposal, they descended upon various points in the United States where they set up depots, organized intricate personnel, managed and stayed with an operation until it was meshed, geared, flawless, and self-performing. Then they retreated to home base, where minds concentrated on the next site of burgeoning business for this enterprising duo. Mousie was a sour little man, dry and humorless, and a teetotaler both of alcohol and drugs. Kiddy Malone was an addict, a small man like Mousie, but outgoing, robust, twinkling-eyed and happy-natured when he was on the stuff—and since he was in the business, he was always on the stuff. Kiddy's Christian name was Kenneth and I was much more intimately acquainted with Kiddy than I was with Mousie Lawrence. Kiddy was an Irishman out of Dublin. Sixteen years ago he had been a seaman who had jumped ship and had remained, without benefit of quota or citizenship, in the United States. Kiddy was a woman's man, and I had first met him when he had got into trouble with his first woman in this country (or second or third or thereabouts). He had been effusively appreciative of my efforts in his be-

half—which was no more than fair since he could not afford
to pay for such efforts at that time in his career—and a
casual acquaintanceship had ripened into a rather ribald and
entertaining friendship, until Kiddy had commenced to sin
with the syndicate, and I had commenced to disapprove of
the new ways and habits of one Kiddy Malone. Before long,
Kiddy's papers were straightened out, a forged citizenship
was forged for him, and he began to patronize the correct
tailors, the correct haberdashers, the correct barbers, the correct booters, and he began to flash bankrolls as thick as
salami sandwiches. He also began to hit the stuff himself—a
mainliner—and he became a personality. Then came Mexico
City, his hookup with Mousie, and the flourishing of a suc-
cessful partnership.

I hailed a cab as I thought about Mousie and Kiddy. If
Mousie was in New York, so was Kiddy, and if they were
in New York, they were working on a deal, and if they were
working on a deal, it was not the kind of deal that Parker
was talking about. Mousie and Kiddy in a mugging act was
as difficult to contemplate as Rogers and Hammerstein doing
words and music for the pornography of a college-boys's stag
party.

Something stank. Out loud.

The cab driver said, "You didn't tell me where to, Jack."

"Nirvana Ballroom," I said. "You know where?"

"I know where," he said and he squinted unpleasantly at
the rear-view.

At Fifty-fifth and Broadway, I paid, alighted, by-passed
Nirvana, and went into a drug store. I bought cigarettes and
gave the man a dollar for change. I took the change to a
phone booth and called Adam Frick's. There was no answer
at Adam Frick's. So I checked the phone book and called
Barbara Phelps. I expected the butler to answer, hoped that
Adam would answer, but Mrs. Phelps came on directly.

"Yes?" she said in a vinegar voice.

"Mrs. Phelps?"

"This is Mrs. Phelps."

"This is Peter Chambers," I said.

"Ah, you have some news for me?" she said.

"Not yet," I said, "but I'm working on it."

"But you called—"

"Is Adam Frick there?"

There was the skip-silence of a moment's hesitation, then, "Yes, he is here, but why——"

"There's a lead on Mr. Phelps," I said. "I need somebody I can trust to help me. I called Mr. Frick at home, he wasn't in, and I thought——"

"Just a moment," she said, "I'll put him on."

Frick said: "Yes, Peter?"

"Hold the receiver close to your ear," I said.

"Yes, Peter."

"I told her I needed you to help me on the Phelps thing. I don't need you for that, but you told me you wanted me to call, so I'm calling. You still want to talk?"

"Yes, Peter."

"You don't mind my bailing you out of there, do you?"

"Not at all, Peter."

"Okay, meet me in . . . an hour. Lorenzo's bar. One hour. Lorenzo's bar."

"A half hour?" he said.

"You want it in a half hour?" I said.

"Yes, Peter."

"Okay. Half hour. Lorenzo's."

"Thank you, Mr. Chambers."

"Don't mention it, Mr. Frick."

I hung up, went out, and once again I paid admission for the privilege of entering into the fragrant dimness of Nirvana. I went immediately to the bar.

"Hi, Mac," said my bartender. "You back already?"

"Who can resist Nirvana?"

"Brother, you're talking. A guy like me behind this bar, he can go out of his mind. Especially I'm married to a gal ain't particular beautiful. A little bit on the ugly side, but you kind of get used to them when they got other things on the ball. You looking for Miss Sierra?"

"Yes," I said.

"Kind of where you left her," he said. "Maybe sopping up the stuff, for all I know. Another sucker bought a bottle, but she got rid of the sucker quick. She ain't in a good mood, if you ask me. What'd you do to her, Mac?"

"Nothing," I said.

"Maybe that's why she ain't in a good mood. Why don't you try again?"

"I'm going," I said.

This time I bought one dollar's worth of tickets and they

were snapped at me with a sniff by the redhead at the box
office. Sniff or no sniff, all I wanted to do was get through
to the roped-off area, and I wanted to get through as in-
expensively as possible as long as the lady in red was not
being impressed this evening by a great show of tickets. I
found her seated at exactly the same table, and alone. She
seemed to be studying the untouched drink in front of her,
but that study was not all-inclusive because she said without
looking up, "Sit down, lover. Glad you're back."

"Didn't know you noticed." I sat opposite.

"I noticed," she said, "and I'm really glad you're back. I
hope you're staying this trip."

"I don't think I am."

"Then why'd you come back?"

"I love you," I said.

"The hell with you," she said, "lover. Have a drink. Glasses
on the tray, bottle under the table and it's Scotch."

I reached and found the bottle. It had hardly been used.
I poured, restored the bottle, said, "You off the stuff?"

"No fun drinking alone. I like to drink with company I
like. You're company I like, but you weren't here. Where
were you, lover?"

"Looking at pictures."

"Looking at pictures?"

"Yeah," I said.

"Clean or dirty pictures?"

"Dirty pictures," I said and brought them out, full face
and profile, and I handed them to her quick-like, all of a
sudden—and I saw her start before she pulled back into
control. "Do you know the guy?" I said.

"No," she said and returned the pictures.

"Ever see the guy?" I put the pictures back in my pocket.

"No," she said.

"Have it your own way," I said and sipped at my drink.

"Have *what* my own way?"

"Skip it," I said. "You're beautiful. I love you."

"Have *what* my own way?" she said.

"You're beautiful," I said.

"Where'd you get those pictures?"

"A friend of mine gave them to me."

"He's no friend of yours."

"Who isn't?"

"Whoever gave them to you," she said. "Give them back."

"Why?" I said.

"They're trouble. Strictly."

"How would you know? You never saw the guy, remember?"

"I'm psychic," she said and smiled with all the beautiful teeth, and I wished I could stay with her.

"I'm going to see your boss," I said.

"And then will you stick around?"

"No, but I'll try to be back."

"Look, let's stop playing shuttlecock. You my date for tonight—or no?"

"Or yes. But I got work to do in between."

"Now look. Either you stick around, or I'm getting out of here. For tonight, I've had it. You're a bad influence. You take my mind off my work."

"I'll try to be back," I said. "Please."

"Well, you're either back real quick, or I'm not here. We'll catch up another night."

"Tonight," I said. "I'll try to be back."

"It's your life," she said. She looked at me, dark-eyed sullen, looked past me. "Don't bother going upstairs for the boss," she said. "He's at the coffee-bar, and he's watching us as if he's expecting us to break a law."

I did not turn to look.

"I'd like to talk to him alone," I said.

"Gentle hint for me to take my fanny elsewhere," she said. "Boy, I could learn to hate you quick."

"It's just I want to talk to him alone," I said.

"The hell with you, lover. If this is your way of trying to put the make on me, maybe you've got the right idea. I'm burning, but I'm still interested. You're a funny joe, but at least you're different. Okay, I'll blow. And if you've got to get out of here, get out right after you talk to Steve. After that, I may wait around a while, but I'm not going to wait around long. You've got things on your mind? Well, so have I." She stood up and kissed the top of my head, lightly. "Good-bye, crazy-joe. The hell with you."

She went away.

Watching her, going away, in that tight red dress, was like watching a conglomerate of all the strip shows on Fifty-second Street. Only better. I cursed her, me, and the business I was in. I reached down for the bottle to add more color to my drink and I saw the well-shod feet stop at my table. I said, still stooped for the bottle, and to impress him with my prowess as a peeper: "Sit down, Stevie. Have a drink. On the house."

I heard his chuckle.

I came up with the bottle in my hand.

"Got eyes in your ass," he said.

"Standard equipment for the private peeper," I said. "Sit down, Stevie. Have a drink."

"Not drinking, thanks," he said. "But I'll sit."

"I'm honored," I said. He sat. I put the bottle back under the table.

"I've been thinking about you," he said.

"And vice versa," I said.

"I mean on that Vivian Frayne deal," he said.

"What do you think I mean?" I said.

He smiled at me.

I smiled at him.

"Maybe I've got a little dope for you," he said.

"I'm always anxious for a little dope," I said.

"Gordon Phelps," he said.

"Maybe that's not all dope," I said.

"Maybe he's more of a dope than you think," he said. "And *he* thinks."

"Like how?" I said.

He sighed, sorrowfully. He sneaked a hand across the table, hooked my drink, and drank from it. "That son of a bitch tried to put me in the middle. Well, I've decided to move over and put him in the middle."

"You mean there's room for both of you?"

"I mean there's room for him."

"Go, boy," I said. "Whoever's in the middle—that's my job."

He sighed again, sorrowfully. "Vivian Frayne knew that George Phillips was Gordon Phelps."

"You tell her?"

"*She* told *me!*"

"Well now, there's a switch. How'd she know?"

"I don't know how she knew."

"Well, why'd she mention it to you?"

"She wanted advice."

"About what?"

"About making it pay off."

"Would you kindly break that down for me," I said, " Mr. Pedi?"

"The fish was on the line," he said. "The bait was swallowed and the hook was through the lip. She had him, but she didn't quite know how to reel him in—and for how much."

"Did you tell her?"

"I don't monkey with that stuff. And if I did, I wouldn't monkey with a dame like Vivian, not with a close deal, not Vivian, you'd never know when she'd go holy-roller on you. Great gal for love that one was, but you didn't monkey with her on a deal, she was too . . . unpredictable."

"The hook was through the lip?" I said.

"She had him. He really went for her. Why, he once even gave her a gun."

"How do you know?"

"She told me."

"What for a gun?"

"There were burglaries in her apartment house. She was leery. A gun is a kind of consolation. A gal like that couldn't get a license for a gun, legitimate. So Phelps lent her his. It made her feel better."

I wondered whether Detective Lieutenant Parker would be as anxious for Phelps if he knew that the gun he had found in the apartment had been there on a kosher lend-lease deal. On the other hand, he might be. The fact that Phelps had lent her the gun for possible defensive purposes did not preclude Phelps' use of the selfsame gun for possible offensive purposes.

"What, exactly," I asked of Steve Pedi, "did Vivian want you to do?"

"She wanted me to move in on it, to take over, to bat the fish over the head and put him into the boat, safe and sound."

"For how much?" I said.

"She figured he'd be good for a hundred thousand big ones."

"And you moved away from that kind of money?"

"That chick was trouble, no matter how much money. I've been around a little. You stay out of deals with a Vivian Frayne."

"You turned her down cold?"

"Yes, sir."

"And she moved along with it—on her own?"

"I'm sure of that."

"So what's that got to do with me, Stevie?"

"I'm putting him in the middle, that's what it's got to do with you."

"Just break that down a little more, please, Stevie."

"Let's say she put the shove on him for a hundred thousand. Let's say he could stand that kind of shove, but let's says he figured it would be the first of many. So, maybe, he doesn't like it. Maybe he hates it. When you've got a hate going, when there's a panic scraping away at you. . . ."

"I'll let you in on a little secret, Stevie."

"Yeah?"

"Vivian was killed by Phelps' gun."

"See what I mean?"

"But would a guy kill a girl with his own gun, and leave the gun there?"

"This guy's no pro in the business. There's an argument, he lets her have it, and he runs. He don't have time to figure angles."

"But the door was locked from the outside. Did he have time to stop for that?"

"Maybe."

"But he claims he has no key."

"So? He claims."

"But that's been verified."

"How?"

"Her diary says the same thing. Phelps had no key."

"Maybe he had a key, and she didn't know about it. Could happen, you know. Maybe he knows what the diary says, so he purposely locks the door—which is almost like an alibi. He says he's got no key, the diary says he's got no key, and the door's locked—so he couldn't have done it. Follow me?"

"Would you testify to all of this, Stevie-boy?"

"Me? I testify to nothing."

"So what's the sense to your telling me?"

"I'm giving you a steer, pal, that's the sense. That old bird tried to put *me* in the middle, didn't he?"

I tried out a smirk on him. (Have you ever tried to smirk?) "He sure did put you in the middle," I said. "Are you copping a plea? Do you say he was lying?"

"Damn right he was lying."

"About your argument with her? Your threat?"

He shoved a thumb at my shoulder. "A hundred percent

snow-job. He was counter-punching, trying to stick me in the middle."

"Well, suppose he says you're lying about this——"

"I'm sure he would, the old son of a bitch."

"So whom do I believe?"

"I don't care whom the hell you believe, pal. The old bum talked first, didn't he? So all right. So I think about it. So I decide I'll do a little rat-job too. He's putting you on me for that murder, so okay, I'm putting you right back on him. Like that we're even up. You can go from there, fella."

"Where do Mousie and Kiddy go?"

"What? What's that?"

Our eyes met across the table like a collision.

"Mousie Lawrence and Kiddy Malone," I said.

"You're using fancy names," he said softly.

"You know them?"

"No," he said. Softly.

"Ever hear of them?"

"Sure," he said. "And I tell you again, fella, you're using fancy names."

"That good?" I said.

"That's bad," he said.

"Why?"

"All I'm saying is you're moving up in class, Mr. Chambers. You move up in class, you're liable to find yourself a hatful of trouble."

"Do you know them, Stevie?"

"No."

"You know how it is," I said.

"What?"

"It gets around to murder, everybody tells a lot of lies, Stevie."

"So maybe it's your job to figure out who's lying."

"That's exactly my job. And to *prove* who's lying."

"Proof?" he said. "That's a cop's job, not your job."

"But that's what I'm getting paid for, Stevie."

"Maybe you can get paid more for letting cops do their own work."

"That an offer, Mr. Pedi?"

"Would you like it to be an offer, friend?"

"No."

"Then it ain't an offer, friend."

"That's what I thought," I said and pushed back from the table and stood up. " 'Bye, Steverino."

"You leaving our attractions?" The capped teeth flashed an ironic smile.

"Reluctantly," I said.

"I think you're nuts," he said.

"Why so?" I said.

"Sierra," he said. "That chick don't flip often. A shame you don't take advantage of it."

"I intend to."

"So why don't you stick around?"

"Believe me, I want to."

"So why don't you?" he said.

"Got to talk to people."

"People talk here, friend."

"I want to go talk to people that talk the truth," I said.

"Don't people here talk the truth?"

"Maybe they do, maybe they don't. I want to go talk to people where I'm sure."

"Where can you be sure, friend?" The smile was almost amiable. "After all, between you and me, where *can* you be sure? I mean, after all, any one of us—who can we talk to that we can be sure?"

"A stoolie, Stevie," I said. "With a stoolie, a right stoolie, if he talks, you can be sure. I'm going to talk to a stoolie, Stevie. Wish me luck. Wish yourself luck."

"Good luck," he said and his soft voice had the flat rasp of a dull knife cutting stale bread.

FOURTEEN

There are stoolies and there are stoolies. There are public stoolies and there are private stoolies, as there are public cops and private cops. Public stoolies are a vital tool of the police. They are little people who do not get sent away for their misdemeanors, and who exchange their meager information for a small form of immunity and a large form of contemptible pride—they wallow in their "connections." They are little men with smidgeons of information which they are happy to use as trade-bait with the police. They are rats, poor, furtive, unintelligent, scurrying around the periphery of the underworld, and frequently discovered as dead clods tossed into a gutter with bullet holes in the mastoid region. These are the public stoolies.

The private stoolie is a completely different breed of the same specie, similar but entirely unlike, as the marauding eagle is unlike the chirping sparrow. The private stoolie is a man (or woman) of brains, perspicacity, discrimination, and a good many bank vaults, all stuffed to capacity. The private stoolie is an encyclopedia of information, a human card-index system, an individual endowed with a peculiar type of genius, and one who cashes in on that. A private stoolie engulfs information as a vulture engulfs carrion: only the stoolie disgorges—for selected individuals at selective prices. He has his own methods and his own means of gathering, reviewing, interpreting, filing and collating his special brand of data—that is his lifework. He is shrewd, dangerous, sometimes deadly. He is rare. He is a specially-gifted specialist in a stratum of society that specializes in specialists. He usually retires, at early middle age, to the bucolic life of gentleman farmer. Or breeder of thoroughbred horses. Or dilettante adventurer in the fabulous realm of the stock market (where this seemingly castrated bull trims the virile bears). Or backer of Broadway hits. Or traveler-about-the-world with a castle in the south of France where the most frantic parties are thrown. But while in action, his fees are more exorbitant than those of the skilled butchers of human flesh called surgeons. And his select clientele numbers senators, statesmen, attorneys, ambassadors, millionaires, royalty, candidates for high office, foreign plenipotentiaries, rulers of state, and, occasionally, upon a lower level of course, a trusted peeper.

I was one of Lorenzo Dixon's clients.

Lorenzo's was a discreet supper club between Park and Madison on Fifty-third Street. It served string music with its victuals—fiddles, zither, and two guitars: imported entertainment as excellent as the food. It was a plush joint that catered to a late crowd. Its cocktail room was black and white with pink lighting overhead; its inner room all pink brocade with candlelight. The inner room had a recessed upstairs gallery, much sought-after by the stay-uppers: it was a mark of distinction (or a mark of a large gratuity to the maître d') to be escorted to the upstairs gallery. It was also a mark of having once been pointed out as a special-type guest by the proprietor of the establishment.

I finger-waved to the maître d' smilingly stationed at the portals of the inner room, but I seated myself opposite Adam Frick at a small round table in the cocktail room. Frick was lost in contemplation of the snifter glass of brandy in front of him and he seemed startled when he glanced up and saw me. He appraised me with eyes as glazed as a windshield in snowtime. Mr. Frick had been punishing the brandy all the way since I had left him, or so it seemed.

"I've been waiting," he said.

"I'm here," I said.

"I'm in trouble," he said.

"I know," I said.

The glazed eyes regarded me fixedly. "You know everything," he grumbled. "A real wise weenie."

"You remind me of a guy," I said. "Amos Knafke."

"You know Amos?" A faint smile stirred in the murk of the eyes.

"We've met," I said.

"Character, huh?" he said and slumped back into unhappiness. "Listen," he said. "You do know my trouble?"

"The cops like you on Vivian Frayne," I said.

"Christ," he said. "How *do* you know? It wasn't in the papers."

"I got a birdie," I said.

"Well, they didn't hold me, did they? They didn't have enough to hold me *on*." He crossed his long legs. "But I'm not out of it," he said morosely. "They'll be grabbing me up again, I know it, I feel it in my bones."

"I'm surprised they didn't hold you," I said. "Really."

"Giving me rope," he said. "Shrewd-apple cops. Giving me rope to hang me."

"They're entitled," I said.

"Why, the sonsabitches? Why? Because I knew the dame? Because I had a key to the place? Because there was a policy for me?"

"It's a lot, and you're not a guy with the most savory of reputations."

He drank from the snifter glass, the edges of it clicking against his teeth. "You want to know something, Petie. I was crazy about that dame, crazy as a guy like me can *be* crazy about a dame. She was something, believe me, something. Why should I want to kill her?"

"You're an angle-guy kid. You'd be coming into twenty-five big ones with her dead."

"I'd be coming into more with her alive."

"Pardon?" I said. "Would you spell that out for me?"

"Look, I'm the guy that steered her on to Phelps."

"Well, now," I said.

"I'd been going with her for some time, real big romance bit. I'd been working for the Phelpses—Mrs. Phelps mostly—"

"Naturally," I said.

"—and when I'd come back from trips, I'd always stop in at the dance hall my first night in town. Well, one night, as I come in there, there's old man Phelps seated at a table with Vivian and another dame, Sophia Sierra. Did you ever meet that one?"

"Yes, sir," I said.

"Well, I sneaked right out of that dance hall, but that night at Vivian's place I told her who he was. He was telling them his name was George Phillips, that kind of crap. I told Vivian to get real cozy with him, that we'd be in a spot to turn a real nice buck, possibly."

"Oh you gentle people," I said.

"Look, a buck's a buck."

"Weren't you making enough bucks from Mrs. Phelps?"

He screwed up his face. "There's no nympho like an old nympho. That Barbara can wear out a battalion."

"I was asking about bucks."

"Three hundred a week, and expenses."

"Big expenses?"

"I earn my keep, Petie. Plus it's like prison. That old bag hardly lets me move."

"I was asking about bucks," I said.

"Let's put it this way," Frick said. "Not enough bucks. Oh, I explored all the possibilities. I mean, like getting married. No soap. She might divorce Phelps, if he got *too* frisky— but she wouldn't marry me."

"Too smart?" I said.

"Yeah, I suppose," he said gloomily. He waved to the waiter for another brandy. The waiter looked inquiringly at

me. I passed. The waiter went away. Frick uncrossed his legs
and nervously teetered one knee. "The old bitch," he said.
"Too smart to want to marry me, but more jealous of me
than of her own husband. She resented Vivian, not because
he was going with her, but because *I* was."

"You mean she knew about Phelps and Vivian?"

"Damn right she knew."

"You mean she kept tabs on him?"

"She kept tabs on me."

"I don't get it," I said.

"She had a peeper on me, Si Murray. He found out about
me and Vivian, and while he was doing the check on me, he
also found out about Phelps and Vivian."

"Busy old Vivian," I said. "But how do you know this?"

"From Si Murray. That's a guy who knows how to work
both sides of the street. Before he made his report to Barbara
Phelps, he double-tracked on her. For two hundred bucks,
he gave me a copy of the report."

"Real trustworthy peeper, eh?"

"They ain't all like you, pal."

"Did Barbara kick up any fuss with you?"

"Nope. She kicked up the fuss with Vivian. She told Vivian
to lay off me. Vivian told her to go to hell. We knew right
then that sooner or later I was going to bust up with the old
bag. That's when we dreamed up the deal to take Gordon
Phelps."

"But if the wife knew about him and Vivian," I said,
"where was the threat?"

A frown put momentary furrows on his smooth forehead.
"Yeah, we thought about that, and there were two answers.
First, maybe he didn't know that the wife knew. And second,
if he did know, we'd kick up a real big stink. Guy goes
prowling dance halls under an assumed name, takes advantage of decent kids, makes all sorts of promises to them,
seduces them, gives them keys to his little hideaway apartment. If he balked on that vacation trip, then we were really
going to put the screws to him. Viv would threaten to go to
the D.A. with a charge of attempted rape—"

"Rape?" I said. "Who's idea was that?"

"Mine," he said innocently. "Anything to raise a stink,
or threaten to raise a stink. Neither Phelps nor Barbara like
stinks like that, big stinks. They're high-class bullshit society
people, you know. Any charge against him would dig up his

. . . his secret life, his maneuvers around the wrong side of the town as George Phillips. We had him by the well-known balls."

"Then why did you want to bring Steve Pedi into it?"

Amazement clouded his face. "How did you know that?"

"I told you before," I said. "I've got a birdie."

He was silent for a moment. Then he said, "We weren't too sure of our ground. Mostly, really, it was me, pushing Vivian. I figured a guy like Pedi would know just how to handle it, and the stake was big enough. I told her to put it up to him, on a three-way split. But he turned her down cold. So we decided to handle it ourselves—that is, she was to handle it. Now do you know what I mean that she was worth more to me alive than dead?"

"You were going to go half on the take from Phelps?"

"Of course. Half of a hundred gees, is fifty. Fifty for me, if she stays alive, is more than twenty-five for me, as she is now—dead. Furthermore, I can't collect a nickel of that unless I get the cops off my back. They don't pay insurance money to the murder suspect."

"Somehow, in your own dirty way, you sound convincing," I said. "If you've got an angle somewhere, you're hiding it pretty good."

He grinned drunkenly. "I've got a bigger angle than you can imagine, and I *am* hiding it pretty good. That's why I wanted to talk to you."

"Well, talk it up, man." Curiosity began biting at me like a flock of mosquitoes.

"Look, there isn't a thing I didn't know about Vivian Frayne, and I'm going to settle this murder thing tonight. I wanted to talk to you first, so you should know what I'm up to."

"What *are* you up to?" I said.

The drunken blue eyes grew crafty. "I'm not telling," he said. "I'm playing a great big hunch, now, tonight. If it works, I'm going to come into a stack of dough, a great big stack of dough. Then I'm going to get me the most expensive lawyer in town to get the heat off me, and I'll also collect on the policy. I'm going to talk to you, and you're going to advise me on a lawyer and all the rest of that, and I'll be able to pay you a handsome fee."

"When are you going to do all this talking to me?"

"You're going to come to my apartment"—he looked at

his watch—"you'll come in an hour, any time after one hour from now. If my hunch pays off, we'll discuss the lawyer angle and stuff. If it doesn't, I'm going to hand you some facts that you're going to take to the cops. Either way, you've got nothing to lose."

He rose, flagged the waiter, paid his check.

He winked at me, raised a fist in salute, and went off.

He was carrying a lot of brandy, but he did not stagger.

FIFTEEN

In the inner room, the maître d' greeted me with the intimate smile generally reserved for the heavy tipper. I tipped him, not heavily enough for the intimate smile, but after all I was there on business, I was not dragging a heavy date and yearning for a secluded table where we could rub knees in private.

"Lorenzo around?" I said.

"Of course, of course," said the maître d'. He escorted me to the gallery and seated me at a corner table, alone. "I shall tell him," he said. "He shall be with you shortly, I am sure."

And shortly, Lorenzo made his appearance, plump in a fastidious dinner jacket, smiling and affable. He was short, fat, smooth and bald, clear gray eyes swimmingly magnified behind the thick lenses of black-rimmed, studious, straight-templed spectacles.

"Ah, Mr. Chambers," he said in a voice like the purr of a cream-fed cat. "Welcome, always welcome." He sat, sighingly, opposite me. "Something to eat? Are you hungry?" He had a round, moon-like face; the fat of an epicure's jowls quivered as he spoke.

"Thanks, Lorenzo," I said. "I'm not hungry."

"A little refreshment?" he inquired.

"Nothing," I said. "I'm on the wagon."

"Mind if I partake? Or would it disturb your wagon?"

"Not at all, Lorenzo. Drink, and be happy."

He waved a pudgy hand at a waiter. "A split of champagne," he said. "Quickly, please. Just one glass. And a tray of hors d'oeuvres."

The champagne appeared. The tray appeared.

Lorenzo sipped and nibbled. I smoked.

"I hope," Lorenzo said, tapping a napkin to his lips, "that I am about to earn some money. You always look nervous when you have to pay money—you're so accustomed to raking it in."

"I look nervous?" I said.

He giggled. "Maybe it's the effects of the wagon?"

"It is not the wagon," I said.

"Then I am breathless in anticipation," he said, and the magnified eyes glittered behind the spectacles. "I hope it's big."

"Not too," I said.

"That's what all my customers say—but, of course, since it is their money, they're prejudiced. I'm prejudiced too, I suppose, but let me be the judge. What is it, Mr. Chambers?"

"Steve Pedi, Mousie Lawrence, Kiddy Malone."

"Together," he said, "or separate?"

"Pedi is separate. Mousie and Kiddy are together."

"Which is as it should be," he said. "On one category, you're going to save money."

"Which category?"

"Pedi," he said.

"Why?" I said.

"Because what I have to offer on Pedi isn't worth any money."

"Will you offer it, please?"

"With pleasure," he said. He sipped champagne. He patted the napkin against his lips. Then he clasped his hands over his stomach. "Stephan Burton Pedi owns a ballroom called the Nirvana. He bought the joint about ten years ago, changed its name to Nirvana, but back then, he didn't operate it himself. He had connections in California, Canada, Florida, and France—some kind of business connections. He'd come in, now and then, and look things over at the Nirvana, but he only took over active operation during the latter part of this past year."

"What kind of business connections?" I said.

"I don't know," Lorenzo said. "He's a very shrewd guy,

a very smart apple, and he sits very strong with some of the best people."

"By the best people, I take it, you mean the worst people."

He shrugged, smiled. "Semantics, a matter of semantics." His hands came off his stomach and he drummed fingers on the table. "He has a couple of relatives who are real big in the organizations. He's fixed tiptop in the connections department. People are afraid of him, the kind of guys who're usually not afraid of anybody. He has a violent temper, and when that gets the better of him, he can be an awfully dangerous man. He's a good guy to stay away from, if you want my advice."

"I'm not here for advice, Lorenzo."

"Naturally not. Well, that's all I know about Steve Pedi, and honestly I just don't want to know too much about that guy. That's my information, my lad—for free."

"What do you know about Mousie and Kiddy, not for free?"

He studied buffed fingernails, then looked up and cocked his head at me. "I don't get you," he said. "This some kind or rib?"

"Pardon?" I said.

"I think you know about as much as I do about those two. Why do you want to throw your money away?"

"I don't want to know about their past history. I want to know about the present. Are they here in New York?"

A pleased smile grew on his face. He was beginning to contemplate earning a fee. "Yes, they're here in New York."

"How long they been here?"

"About a month, I think."

"Why are they here?"

"I don't know."

"You slipping, Lorenzo?"

"Lorenzo doesn't slip. They're only here a short time. I don't know just why they're here—yet. I'll know, sooner or later, but I don't know yet. You want to be in touch with either one of them?"

"I want to be in touch with both of them."

He rubbed his hands together. "Now we're on much firmer ground," he said. "Is it important to you?"

In the age-old manner of every purchaser looking to keep the price down, I lifted my eyebrows and shrugged my shoulders.

"It's important to you," Lorenzo announced, "or you wouldn't be here. A thousand bucks does it."

"Are you kidding?"

"Lorenzo doesn't kid. You know that."

"But a thousand bucks! For what?"

"For information as to where they're staying, under what names they're staying, plus information about the brand new gal Kiddy's palsy-walsy with."

I grabbed an hors d'oeuvre and munched. I knew Lorenzo. The guy could be as stubborn as a wing collar. When Lorenzo set a price, you take it or leave it. I took it.

"Deal," I said.

"Delighted," he said. "I'll call at your office tomorrow for payment."

"You won't have to trouble yourself," I said. I took out Barbara Phelps' check, endorsed it, and handed it over.

He looked at it, nodded, folded it away. "You must be clairvoyant," he said, "coming with exactly the correct amount of buckshot."

"It's swindle-money," I said. "Maybe in a way I'm glad to get rid of it."

"Well, I'm glad you're getting rid of it here. I have no compunctions, as long as it's money." His jowls shook as he chuckled without sound.

"Okay, enough with the patter," I said. "You're paid. Talk it up."

"Of course, dear Peter." He sat back and clasped his hands once again over his stomach. His eyes rolled up to the ceiling; and then the lids came down and he sat as though communing with the spirits. He was thinking. I let him think. Then the words came. "Mousie Lawrence," he said, "is Emanuel Larson. Kiddy is Kenneth Masters. They have a suite at the Montrose Hotel, Fifty-seventh and First, Suite 916."

"Charming," I said. "Now the bonus."

"Bonus?" he said, his eyes still closed.

"Kiddy's girl friend."

"Oh yes," he said. "She's a waitress in a fish restaurant on Fulton Street called Old Man Neptune. She's a redhead with a terrific shape. If I ever got my mind off eating, she's the type I'd like to make myself. She's a gal who ought to be in a pleasant mood these days, because she's a junkie and Kiddy keeps her well supplied with the stuff. Name, Betty Wilson; three-room apartment at 244 West 65th Street, first floor, rear apartment to the right. There are four apartments on each floor, two in front and two in the rear; it's an old brownstone, a walkup, and you don't have to ring downstairs if you don't want to because the entrance door is on the fritz and it doesn't snap shut on its lock." He opened his eyes. "Okay?"

"Wow," I said in wonderment.

He blinked smiling eyes at me. "Leave it to Lorenzo."

"Wow," I said and I stood up. "Happy-happy with the swindle-money. I enjoyed the demonstration." He extended his hand and we shook. I said, "Please remember, I only dropped in to say hello. I didn't inquire about anybody."

"Leave it to Lorenzo," he said.

SIXTEEN

The Montrose was one of those newly-built thousand-room monstrosities, tier upon jagged tier of stone, chrome, brick and steel. I stalked through the lobby as though I belonged and a shiny-doored elevator took me up to nine. I marched to 916, put my finger on the doorbell and squeezed.

Nothing happened. I continued to squeeze the doorbell and nothing continued to happen. I marched back to the elevator and rode down to the main floor. I was quite anxious for a look-see into Suite 916. I was right there on the premises and you never can tell what a look-see can turn up, even a fast look-see. If the boys were there—just not answering the bell —well, old Pete was an old friend, and maybe we could work out a little chatter: I might even discuss a fingerprint the cops had laboriously developed on a knife dropped by a mugger. If the boys were not there, I'd have my look-see. I am an old hand in my racket. You press every angle. You push every button. You go through every door.

I strode quickly to the desk.

It was long and wide with a white marble top. There were five clerks behind it, two busy, and three trying to look busy with nothing to do (which is a neat trick if you can pull it). I started yelling almost as soon as I got there. I reached across and grabbed tha lapel of one of the three, a kid with a butch haircut, a white face, and a black bow tie.

"I'm Larson!" I yelled. "Jack Larson! I'm Larson!"

"What the hell?" said the white-faced kid.

"I got a brother here! Emanuel Larson! 916!"

"So what?" said the white-faced kid. "Let go, will you, Mac?"

One of the others moved near, a portly, gray-haired man with glasses. "What is wrong?" said the gray-haired man.

"My brother called me!" I shouted. "Called me, threatening suicide!"

"Suicide," breathed the gray-haired man.

"Let go the jacket," implored the white-faced kid.

"I tried to call here, but your gahdamned switchboard operator must be asleep!" I yanked at the lapel. "Let's get moving, Mac!"

"You sure he called from here?" said the gray-haired man.

"I don't know where the hell he called from! He called! He lives here! 916! Now let's get a move on! Please!"

The gray-haired man said, "There is a Larson in 916."

"Yes there is," said the kid I was holding. He moved abruptly, wrenching loose from my lapel-hold. "916," he said to the gray-haired man who was moving away. "Emanuel Larson and Kenneth Masters."

The gray-haired man took a ring of keys and came out from behind the desk.

"This way," he said to me. "Come along, please."

He was sprightly for a fat man. We ran across the lobby and into an elevator.

"Nine," he said to the elevator boy, "and no other stops."

Upstairs, he opened the door of 916. All the lights were on. We went through a small square foyer into a large square sitting room. It was an expensive suite. The sitting room was expensively furnished: floor-to-ceiling casement windows, velvet draperies, ankle-deep carpet, gilt-framed mirrors, sound-proofed walls, artful adornments tastefully disposed—except for one unexpected adornment, rigid in the middle of the ankle-deep carpet, which completely destroyed the decor of the room: Mousie Lawrence, fully dressed, and very dead. He lay, face up and hideous, his upper lip a red gaping hole.

The lower half of his face was a mass of dried blood, crusted and scaly, broken teeth gleaming in a bullet-destroyed grin. His eyes were open in an unblinking fish-stare. Forehead and ears were stamped with the wax-yellow of death.

Retchingly, the gray-haired man gasped as he bent to examine him. I did not bend to examine him. A private richard is like an embalmer: he has seen enough of death to recognize it instantly. Instead, I went through to the bedroom. That, too, was brilliantly lighted, but it was uninhabited. A shoulder-holster, with pistol, was on the bed. Another holster, belt-type, and also with pistol, hung on the back of a chair. I examined both pistols. They were fully loaded.

I returned to the sitting room. The gray-haired man was latched to the phone, chanting, "Yes, yes, dead, dead, Mr. Larson. . . ."

I went to the door.

The gray-haired man cupped his palm over the mouthpiece and called to me: "Sir! Sir! Where are you going? Just a moment!"

"I'm going to the cops," I said.

"I'm arranging for that right now."

"Arrange," I said. "You arrange your way. I'll arrange mine. I'm going for the cops, and the hell with you and worrying about bad publicity for the hotel."

He was back on the phone.

"No, please," he was saying. "No excitement. Have the girl call, there are very few people in the lobby at this time. . . ."

I went out, and down in the lobby I was met by two of the desk clerks in the company of a very tall, lean, dignified man in a black suit. "This is the manager," one of the clerks said. "This is Mr. Hopkins. We were just going up——"

"Go up," I said. "I can't stay up there."

"Of course, of course," Mr. Hopkins commiserated.

The three of them went into an open elevator, Hopkins said, "Nine, quickly" to the elevator boy, and I walked across the lobby into the street.

I walked, aimlessly, until I found a hamburger joint. I had coffee and smoked cigarettes and tried to paste a few of the pieces together. Whoever had killed him had been a friend. Guys like Mousie and Kiddy didn't keep their artillery in the bedroom unless they were entertaining a friend in the sitting room—a friend—someone whom they trusted—that is, unless it was Kiddy himself who had put the blast on Mousie. That sort of thing has happened before: they both toss off their holsters, but one of them has an extra piece on his person, and that is the piece he uses to put a splash on the ankle-deep carpet and spoil the decor of the sitting room. But why should Kiddy Malone kill Mousie Lawrence? Then again, why not? People fall out, especially animals of the stripe of Kiddy and Mousie, and I could inquire into that because I knew where to catch up with Kiddy Malone. All the Kiddy Malones, since the time of Cain, hole up, in a moment of fright, in the self-same place: the abode of the mother symbol. They scurry to the comfortable cocoon of the soft-enveloping arms of a convenient female. Don't they all? Turn an eye to page three of the tabloids! Every lamster has to be shot to death or tear-gassed out of the apartment, the shack, the house, the bungalow, the cottage, the love-nest of his dearly-beloved. And I knew of the most recent of Kiddy Malone's dearly-beloveds. And Kiddy Malone did not know that I knew, or that anyone knew, about this most recent dearly-beloved, because no one, especially not Kiddy, could have any possible idea as to the remnants of off-beat information which were within the peculiar ken of a genius named Lorenzo Dixon. Kiddy had only been in town about a month, and Lorenzo had said that Betty Wilson was a brand new girl friend, so where else would Kiddy Malone be? And there was no rush. I had time. Mousie Lawrence, from the blood-crust on him, had been dead for quite a number of hours. So there was no rush. I had time. I wanted Kiddy Malone well bedded-down before I called upon him. I sighed, grunted, pressed out my cigarette, mopped up the dregs of my coffee. I looked at my watch. It was an hour and ten minutes since I had talked with Adam Frick.

SEVENTEEN

The Wadsworth Arms was a sprawling oldtimer on West End Avenue near Ninetieth Street. Thirty years ago, West End

Avenue had been the Park Avenue of the West Side; today
it had grown old and shabby and the Wadsworth Arms had
grown old and shabby with it. When my cab was stopped for
a light at Ninetieth Street, I said, "All right, this will do,"
paid, got out, and strolled toward the Wadsworth Arms. A
woman emerged, looked about hurriedly, and walked in the
direction away from me. The cab, cruising, caught up with
her, and its horn honked gently, as it moved to the curb beneath a street lamp. The woman turned, and entered the cab,
but she had stopped for a moment beneath the street lamp
and I had recognized her. It was Mrs. Barbara Phelps. The
cab started, picked up speed, and turned the corner. I stood
quite still for a moment, finished my cigarette, and flung it
into the gutter. Then I proceeded to the Wadsworth Arms.

Its tall, graceful, downstairs doors had grown ancient and
rickety and were unlocked. The marble of the spacious inner
lobby was cracked and the rugs were color-drained and
threadbare. There were wall brackets with light bulbs, a few
tables, and lamps upon the tables. The light bulbs had metal
protectors around them so that they could not be unscrewed
and stolen. The lamps were chained to the tables. The Wadsworth Arms now catered to a furnished-room clientele and,
it appeared, they did not trust their customers, or, at least,
were distrustful of the vandals of the neighborhood. There
were three elevators, two of which bore "not working" signs.
The third was open on the lobby floor, a self-service contrap-
tion with paneled mirrors, one of which was missing. I pushed
the six button because Adam Frick's furnished apartment
was 6B. The elevator lurched and creaked like an elderly
wife trying to impress a young husband. It jolted to a stop at
six, and I got out safe and sound. I walked to 6B and was
about to push the button when I noticed the door was ajar.
Presentiment shimmered through me like a chill. I pushed at
the door with my foot. It swung open silently.

The place was fully lighted. I stepped across the threshold and stood still, listening. I was in a small foyer. Inside,
there seemed to be a faint rasping sound. It was indefinable
—a faint rasping sound. I moved the door back, leaving it as
I had found it, slightly ajar, and straining my ears to the
sound, I went forward, carefully.

Adam Frick was in the living room. He was seated in an
easy chair, his head lolling, his eyes closed, blood leaking

from his mouth. The faint rasping sounds were emanating from him—a weak, gurgling wheeze from his throat.

I went to him swiftly, tilted his chin back.

He had been shot through the neck, blood still spurting from a jagged hole, and he had been shot through the left side of the chest, blood a sickening red formless stain on his shirt.

Just then his eyes opened.

And he recognized me.

"Pete." It was supplication. *"Pete."*

I took his face in my hands and held it firm.

There was nothing I could do. The man was dead. He was dead right now though his heart was still pumping the blood out of him.

"Easy, kid," I said. "Easy does it, Adam."

It was amazing that he knew me. Dying as he was, final death in his eyes, the brain still functioned in recognition.

"Pete!"

He said my name again and then the gurling rasp became a rattle. A convulsive movement of the body threw it upward and it held, rigidly, and then it went limp and sank to the chair. The rattle persisted, and then the eyes opened, opened wide, and the blue glazed eyes had intelligence, and he said clearly, "The wife," and then the rattle was a faint sighing whistling, and he murmured, "Wife . . . wife . . ." and then the blue eyes rolled up, and the head grew heavy in my hands, and he was dead.

And then I heard the door kicked open, and there was the tramp of many feet, and the place was flooded with cops.

EIGHTEEN

The technical boys had completed their tasks, the photo boys had clicked off their work, the ambulance-man had officially declared the remains a corpse, and the basket boys had removed the body—the police routine was done and finished.

Detective Lieutenant Parker had given his orders, the army of cops had retreated to their jobs downtown, and Adam Frick's apartment contained but the two of us, Parker and myself, Parker seated in the selfsame easy chair in which I had found Adam Frick. We were each of us—illegal heirs to Adam Frick's Scotch—sipping from tall glasses.

"Okay," Parker said. "Let's have it."

"Am I to consider myself under arrest or something?" I said.

"Don't be silly," Parker said. He ignited a fresh cigar. "But don't make *me* look silly. Please."

"I don't quite get that," I said.

"Don't, don't you?" Parker puffed fragrant blue smoke. "Now look. We come in here and find you with a dead guy, blood all over you. Okay, you washed up, and you're nice and clean now. There's no gun on you, nothing like that, but still, we find *you*—and the dead guy. I've got to make a report, and you've got to be in my report. So . . . kindly don't make me look silly. Give me the stuff for my report. Kindly, if you please."

"What brought you?" I said.

"Pardon?" he said.

"Suddenly there were cops," I said.

"Oh, that," he said. "Somebody somewhere picked up a telephone, got an operator, said, 'I want a hospital, emergency.' The operator put them through to the Polyclinic. The somebody said to the switchboard of the Polyclinic, 'A man has been shot, emergency,' and gave them this address, apartment 6B. The somebody hung up—which makes it what's known as an anonymous call—and the switchboard girl, at once, called it in to the police, which is routine. That's how we got here and the ambulance got here practically together with us. Now, please, how the hell did you get here?"

"Adam Frick invited me."

"When?"

"Tonight."

"Where? How? What?"

"I ran into him, a couple of hours ago, at Lorenzo's, at the cocktail lounge. He was slightly swacked on brandy. He said he wanted to talk to me."

"He had trouble?" Parker said, heavily ingenuous.

"He might have had," I said quite innocently.

"You mean he needed a private eye because he'd got

locked up once in conjunction with the murder of Vivian Frayne?"

"He said he wanted to talk to me about Vivian Frayne."

"Couldn't he have talked to you right there where he was?"

"Am I one to dispute the whim of a prospective client, Lieutenant?"

"And just what was the whim?" the Lieutenant inquired.

"He asked me to come here to his apartment. Said he wanted to have discourse with me. Asked me to give him about an hour or so, and come here."

"And you came here—when?"

"About five minutes prior to your finding me—with his head in my hands."

"How'd you get in?"

"About the same as you got in, Lieutenant. The door was slightly open, and I left it that way. He was sitting in the chair you're sitting in now. He was dying, a bullet through his neck, and one through his chest—I found him the way you saw him."

"I saw him dead."

"And I saw him just next to dead."

"Anything else, Peter?"

"That's about it, Louis. I'm very curious about that anonymous call."

"*You're* curious." He stood up. "I'd like you to come in with me, so we can get a formal statement from you on this thing. Okay?"

"Certainly," I said.

A young cop was a lone sentinel outside the door and Parker told him to go in. "Any calls or callers," Parker told him, "you know how to handle them. Take any messages and get them through to us. A caller in person, whoever it is, I want to talk to him. Or her."

"Yes, sir," the young cop said.

"There's some whiskey," Parker said. "You can have a snort or two, but don't make a pig of yourself."

"Yes, sir," said the young cop, restraining a smile.

"Okay, Pete, let's go," Parker said.

We drove to the precinct house in silence. Once, Parker said, "What did you think of Frayne's apartment?"

I said, "I haven't been there yet."

He wafted a frown at me, continued driving, and then we were at the station house, and in his office two detectives were waiting in the company of a short woman with a back-side as wide as an artist's viewpoint.

"From the switchboard at the·Poly," one of the detectives said.

"Ah, Miss . . . Miss . . ." Parker said.

"Mrs.," the lady said. "Mrs. Rebecca Reilly."

"Yes, Mrs. Reilly," Parker said. "About that phone call that came through to you, the emergency——"

"Your boys already quizzed me on that, sir."

"He's Lieutenant Parker," one of the detectives said.

"Already quizzed me, Lieutenant Parker."

"Good, good," Parker said. "They didn't give a name, did they?"

"No, sir, Lieutenant."

"Man's voice or woman's voice?"

"Woman's voice, sir."

"Remember what she said?"

"Said something like: 'Man's been shot, emergency. Wadsworth Arms on West End Avenue. Apartment 6B.' Then she hung right up."

"And what did you do?"

"Called it in to our emergency downstairs, you know, where the wagon is, the ambulance. Then called it right in to the cops."

"Good, good," Parker said. "Now was there anything special about the woman's voice?"

"No, sir, Lieutenant. A woman's voice."

"Your emergency turned out to be a murder, Mrs. Reilly. Anything special, anything distinctive, about that woman's voice may be of great help to us. Please think, Mrs. Reilly."

"I already thought, Lieutenant. She talked fast, is all, and hung up before, practically, I had a chance to breathe. But that's all, sir. There weren't anything special, no sir, not a thing, just a woman's voice talking in a hurry."

Parker threw her a dim glance, nodded shortly, said, "Thank you very much. My boys will take you out to have a formal statement dictated and signed. And, oh, gentlemen, this is Peter Chambers. He's got a statement for the stenographer too."

They took us to another room, Rebecca Reilly and me, and there we dictated our respective statements, and waited until they were typed, and then we read them and signed them and had our signatures witnessed, and then Mrs. Rebecca Reilly was permitted to go back to sitting in front of her switchboard, and I returned to Parker's office.

He was at his desk, brooding over two small pellets and one large typewritten sheet. "Crime," he murmured, "it's crazy."

"Yes, sir, Lieutenant," I said in my best Rebecca Reilly manner.

He snapped out of it, smiled wanly. "Okay on the statement?" he said.

"A hundred percent fine," I said. "I was succinct and grammatical. I did you proud."

Wistfully he looked at the pellets and sheet. "Crime . . ." he began.

"What's crazy?" I said.

"Go get the hell out of here."

"You mean I'm discharged, Lieutenant?"

But his gaze remained upon the objects on his desk.

"Lieutenant," I said, "confession is good for the soul. Talk eases the mind. Remember me? I'm your boy."

He lifted the two pellets, clenched them in a fist, squinted at me. "How well did you know Adam Frick?"

"Pretty well."

"Do you know if he was acquainted with Mousie Lawrence?"

"Offhand, I'd say no." I squinted right back at him. "What's crazy, Lieutenant?" I tried to make it sound casual but it came out with goose-bumps.

"There are things that happen," he said with a faint touch of malice in his voice, "that even you don't know."

"Yes, sir," I said meekly.

"Not many things," he amended. "Some things."

"Yes, sir," I said meekly.

"You wouldn't figure to know that this happened. It hasn't hit the papers yet."

"What happened?" I said.

"Remember the Mousie Lawrence we talked about earlier today?"

I'd fill him in on my part later on. This was not the time. I still had a Kiddy Malone to work on.

"Yes, sir," I said.

"Mousie Lawrence was murdered."

"No," I said.

"Yes," he said. "Okay, a mug like that gets killed, he gets

killed. But you wouldn't think that the world of Mousie
Lawrence and the world of Adam Frick had any connection,
now would you?"

"I wouldn't," I said.

"Neither would I," he said. "A professional like this
Mousie, and a wise-guy snot-nose like this Frick, you'd figure
them worlds apart, wouldn't you?"

"I would," I said.

He opened his fist and showed me the pellets. "Slugs
out of Adam Frick." He pointed to the typewritten sheet on
the desk. "Ballistic report," he said. "How crazy can it get?"

"Crazy like how?" I said.

"The bullets we pried out of the bodies of each of them,"
Parker said, "were discharged from the selfsame gun." And
he squinted again and scowled, thinking, as he scratched a
hand through the scrub of his hair. "Please," he said, "get
the hell out of here. We've got work to do."

NINETEEN

It was somewhat late for making a social call at a mansion
on upper Fifth Avenue but there I was, making the call, my
finger pressed to a large white bell. There was no answer but
I persisted, rigid digit firm, patient as that hero of yesteryear
with his finger stuck in the dike. The patience of this year's
hero was finally rewarded by a sound within: a scrape of
metal. Then the door opened against a chain-latch, giving a
spread of about four inches, and I was greeted by one peer-
ing eye and the two nostrils of a nose. The British accent, entirely unruffled, inquired, quite mildly, "Yes, what is it,
please?"

"I'm to see Mrs. Phelps."

Either the eye recognized me or the nostrils smelled me.
"Ah, Mr. Chambers." Then the British accent was muffled by
lugubrious overtones. "So late, late, it is rather late, don't you
think, sir?"

"Yes I think. But it's important. Is she asleep?"

"No, sir, I don't believe so. Though I was."

"Please forgive me," I said. "But if she's up, she could have come to the door herself, couldn't she?"

"Mrs. Phelps never comes to the door, sir."

"Then blame her, don't blame me."

"I'm not blaming anyone, sir. You insist it's important?"

"Not insisting, really. Just stating."

"If you'll please wait, sir, I'll go inquire."

"Thank you."

The door was closed in my face, but gently.

Minutes later, it was opened, all the way.

The butler was sleepy-eyed and wrapped within a blanket of bathrobe but the old boy had the knack: he was quite as dignified as though he were in tails. "Mrs. Phelps is in the drawing room, sir, you know where it is. You'll pardon me if I don't escort you. Good night, sir."

"Good night," I said. "I'm sorry I woke you."

"Not at all, sir, not at all."

He smiled, nodded, turned, and disappeared through an archway on the right. I went to my left, to the drawing room, now softly lit by candles. She was waiting for me in the middle of the room, strikingly handsome in the candlelight. She was wearing black silk high-necked lounging pajamas. She was taller than I had thought, standing regal and imperious, alone in the room. She looked good, the blue-gray hair swept back in a youthful ponytail, the large proud brown eyes insolently appraising me, every point and curve of her revealed in the black silk pajamas, and the lady had excellent points and excellents curves. She was still on the brandy although she had switched from the bulbous curves of a snifter glass to the more serviceable straight lines of a water tumbler which, at this moment, half-full, she held in her right hand.

"A nocturnal rendezvous," she said. "To what do I owe the pleasure, Mr. Chambers?"

Even her voice was different, vibrant and with a curious husky excitement in it.

"I have a report for you," I said.

"Couldn't it have waited?" she said.

"Would you have wanted it that way?"

"I think this is exactly the way I want it," she said, and she smiled, and I noticed her teeth, bright-white and even, and her lips, red-wet and glistening. I was suddenly very much aware of her and she seemed to sense it. "I have an announcement to make to you, Mr. Chambers," she said, "before you make your report to me."

"Announcement?" I said.

"I am very drunk," she said.

"You certainly don't appear to be," I said.

"That's my curse," she said. "The drunker I get, the more sober, it seems, do I act. I don't even stagger, damn it. Oh, in the end, I fall down, I just curl up and collapse. But until then I remain very much the lady except for uncontrollable impulses." She set the glass down on a table and came near me, without a stagger.

"Impulses?" I said.

"Something like this," she said. She put her arms around me and kissed me. My hands hung at my sides, but not for long. Her mouth was hot, her lips soft, her tongue inquisitive and experienced. My arms came up around her and pressed her to me. Her body was softly feminine, but strong, and there was a fragrance about her. Her knee moved up between the two of mine and she wriggled and we clung like that and I had a sudden vision of becoming a private pilot at three hundred dollars a week and expenses although I had not the slightest idea as to what makes an airplane tick, let alone fly. And then her mouth moved to my ear and she whispered, "This has been on my mind since late this afternoon. You're a very attractive man, Mr. Chambers." And then she let go and backed off and the insolent eyes appraised me again and she said, "Too bad you don't drink, Mr. Chambers."

"Who said that?" I gasped.

"You did," she said, "this afternoon."

"Well, I've learned since then."

"Help yourself," she said and waved toward the bar. And as I poured, she said, "Adam told me you were a liar. He said you drink like a fish, more power to you."

"Let's talk about Adam," I said.

Her chin went up. "Let's have your report first."

"Your husband's all right," I said. "He's here in town."

"Did you tell him to call me?"

"He'll call you."

"Well, he hasn't yet."

"He will," I said. "Let's talk about Adam."

She lifted her tumbler, held it out to me, smiled, and drank. "First, please," she said, "let me make a small speech. Adam Frick was a charming young scoundrel who amused me for a while. When I'm amused, I'm vitally interested. But with the Adam Fricks, that passes. Adam was young and beautiful, but quite dull. For instance, you're not quite as young nor quite as beautiful as Adam Frick, but you're much more of a man, and I'm certain you'd never be dull. A man like you could be dangerous for a woman like me."

"And Adam Frick?"

"Adam Frick passed out of my life today. Suddenly, I was sick and tired of Adam Frick, and sick and tired of myself for ever having been interested in Adam Frick."

"He's dead, Mrs. Phelps."

"I know," she said, "and frankly it doesn't mean a thing to me. Adam Frick was destined to die violently and in the prime of his youth. He was a wretched, evil young man who constantly played cat and mouse with death. That's a losing game, Mr. Chambers."

"Now just a minute," I said.

"Do I sound heartless? Honestly, I don't mean to." She drank from her tumbler. "But I'm not a child, Mr. Chambers. The fact of death, the inevitable fact of death, simply doesn't frighten me, and I cannot be hypocritical about these things. I've seen a good deal of death in my lifetime, Mr. Chambers. There are some whom I've mourned, and others whom I haven't. Adam Frick is dead and I do not mourn him and I shall make no pretense that I do."

"And suppose I tell you that you may be involved in this death—involved, as far as the authorities are concerned?"

"I would regret that, of course." She came near me again. "And now, please, would you tell me how you know he is dead, and how you know I may be involved in it?"

"Hang on to your brassiere straps, Mr. Phelps. We do it my way, if you please."

She smiled. "You see what I mean about your not being dull."

"Let's start with Vivian Frayne," I said.

"The lady whom my husband is suspected of murdering?"

"You may be suspected yourself, Mrs. Phelps."

"Am I?"

"Not yet."

"But I may be? When?"

"When I'm finished saying my piece. To the police."

"Oh now," she said and kissed my lips lightly. "Do I smell a little blackmail?"

"You don't smell a thing, Mrs. Phelps. Except, perhaps, yourself."

"Touché," she said. "I deserved that." She chuckled. "You're certainly not dull, Mr. Chambers. Watch out. I think I'm falling in love with you."

"I'm watching," I said. "Let's get back to Vivian Frayne. You kind of hated her, didn't you?"

"Temporarily. During my early infatuation with Adam."

"I know all about that."

"I assume you do, Mr. Chambers. I assume Adam confided in you. But at the time of Miss Frayne's death, my affections for Adam were on the wane. I can't honestly say she was important enough any more for hatred."

"Look, Mrs. Phelps. I was here this afternoon. I saw the way you looked at Adam."

"You may have been confusing passion with disgust. Both are strong emotions."

She was either brilliantly clever or unthinkably honest.

"I talked with him here on the phone," I said. "I had to use subterfuge to get him out of here."

"On his say-so, wasn't it, Mr. Chambers?"

"Yes, on his say-so."

"As a matter of fact, I would have been delighted to have had him out of here, the quicker the better. But his stupid male ego didn't permit him to tell that to you. He was here because he wanted to be here. He was trying to negotiate a loan from me. He wanted money in order to retain a skilled lawyer. He had been arrested and released in connection with Vivian Frayne's death. He was still a suspect."

"I know all about that," I said.

"About his trying to borrow money from me?"

"No. About his being arrested and released. Now please listen to me carefully, Mrs. Phelps."

"I'm listening, Mr. Chambers."

"I got him out of here," I said.

"On the pretense that he would assist you in locating my husband. That *was* a pretense, wasn't it, Mr. Chambers?"

"Yes."

"Of course. Please go on."

"We got together, Adam and I. He had some clear-cut

idea as to the murderer of Vivian Frayne. He was to see that person, and have it out, once and for all, tonight. And then he was going to tell me about it; at least something about it, one way or another. Were you that person, Mrs. Phelps?"

"Categorically—no!"

"But you did go to visit him tonight, didn't you?"

Sharply she said, "How do you know that?"

"I saw you," I said.

She was silent, gnawing at a corner of her mouth between her teeth.

"I saw you come out of there," I said. "You took the very same cab I had gotten out of. I was up in his apartment within three minutes. I found him dying, shot through the neck and chest. Did you kill him, Mrs. Phelps?"

"Categorically—no!"

"Do you want to talk to me about it, Mrs. Phelps?"

"Are you going to talk to the police?"

"I have every intention to."

"Have you?"

"Not yet."

"And when do you—have every intention to?"

Now I sipped my drink, stalling for time, collecting my thoughts, making up my mind. "Tomorrow," I said. "Tomorrow, I intend to bring your husband in, and I intend to relieve myself of everything I know about the death of Vivian Frayne and the death of Adam Frick." I tried a long shot. "And the death of Mousie Lawrence."

"Who's that?" she said.

"Nobody," I said. "Precisely, nobody."

"Why tomorrow?" she said.

"Because tonight I'm still glorious unto myself, the private richard bumbling along in his private investigation, building his ego, and hoping for the best. Are you the one Adam had a date with?"

"No."

"Then what were you doing there?"

She poured more brandy into her glass. "Let's say I was drunk, acting on one of my impulses. I've been drinking most of the day, please remember."

"What impulse?" I said.

"I wanted to tell Adam off, once and for all. I simply didn't want him back here, ever. I decided to go over to his place and tell him."

"How'd you get in?"

"I have a key, of course."

"The door was slightly open when I got there."

"I probably didn't slam it in my hurry to leave. It's that kind of door, shuts on a slam."

"And did you tell him off, Mrs. Phelps?"

She smiled, sweetly. "You trying to trap me, Mr. Chambers?"

"Just asking, Mrs. Phelps."

"No, I didn't tell him off," she said. "I got there, rang the bell, there was no answer. I decided to go in and wait for him. I opened the door, went in, and there he was in that easy chair, shot, gurgling, dying. I didn't want to be involved in it, of course. There was nothing I could do to help him, nothing."

"Yes, I'll buy that," I said.

"The quickest way to get any kind of help to him would be an emergency call to a hospital. I used his phone, and did exactly that. And then I left. Please believe me, Mr. Chambers."

"I'm trying to. Honestly."

"Look, if I'd have had anything to do with it, would I have called the hospital?"

"Who said *you* called the hospital?"

She stared at me blankly for a moment. "But who else?"

"I don't know," I said. "Possibly, you. Probably, you. I don't know. I'll say this. If it turns out that you're telling the truth, I'll do my level best to keep you out of it. The cops are working on it right now, and me, I'm still working on it. If either one of us catches up with whoever dunit— and that whoever is not you—I promise you that I won't involve you in it, I'll never mention your name, there'd be no reason to, and concealing a little information like that harms no one."

"Thank you. You're awfully sweet."

"Well, that's about it, Mrs. Phelps."

"Is it?" she said, and there were tears in her eyes, and she smiled a faint, queer, lovely, enigmatic smile. She was near to me and she touched me.

I tried very hard to be faithful to Sophia Sierra.

TWENTY

I strolled toward Madison for a taxicab. I thought about returning to the Nirvana but rejected that. I found a cab and said, "115 East 64th." I was going to Vivian Frayne's but I kept thinking about Barbara Phelps. She was either the most straightforward woman I had ever met or she was more twisted than a prize case out of Freud. I had been certain that she was it as far as Adam Frick was concerned, and if she had done Frick, she would also have been involved with Mousie's murder, since both of them got it from the same gun. I had been certain that Adam himself had tipped me when he had gasped, "Wife . . . wife." Wife? Who else but Gordon Phelps' wife? What other wife did we know in common? I had been certain—but now I was no longer certain. She had parried every thrust, she had wriggled out of every trap; and her very demeanor—she was either a natural-born actress, or the brandy served as insulation against guilt, or she was telling the truth. I shrugged, lonely in my corner of the cab. This was for Parker, not for me. This was for the public cop, not the private cop. And I thought about Parker, lovely man. We had been together for a long time this night —at Adam Frick's, at Parker's office—and not once had he mentioned Gordon Phelps. I had promised to deliver Phelps within twenty-four hours, and Parker depended upon that; if Phelps were to have come into our discussion, I would have had to bring him up. We had made a trade, Parker and I; I had Vivian Frayne's keys in my pocket to prove it, and I had quite a good many confidential facts. Well, he would have Gordon Phelps within twenty-four hours, and he might have Mrs. Phelps to boot. And he'd have all of *my* confidential facts.

"115 East 64th," said the cabbie.

"Yes, sir," I said and I paid and I went into a narrow lobby and Parker's keys were as efficacious as penicillin in a bordello. Everything worked smoothly. A gander at the bell-brackets produced FRAYNE at 4G. One key opened the downstairs door, and another key opened the door of 4G. There was no fuss, there was no fight, there were no balky door locks. I put on the lights and I approved, noddingly, as I stalked about, appreciative as a geologist in a newly-blasted cave. Vivian Frayne, before the bullets, had done very much of all right for herself. The two-room apartment was as sumptuous as the promise of a politician. The layout was more than a two-room apartment. The foyer was a room in itself; then there was a three-step-down living room, expansive and high-ceilinged; then a fine wide spacious bedroom; then a kitchenette that was diminutive only in comparison to the vastness of the other rooms. There were nooks and alcoves which in themselves were additional rooms, and there was an awninged, tile-floored terrace outside the bedroom. The apartment was a delight, but my intensive inspection of it added not one whit to my investigation into the death of its occupant. So, I had seen Vivian Frayne's apartment. So, I had played detective and inspected the scene of the crime. Three cheers for me. I put out the lights in all the rooms, and I was just about to switch the foyer light, when I heard the sound.

Somebody was poking at the lock.

I flicked out the light and, in darkness, I waited behind the door. I breathed deeply, through an open mouth, trying to tranquilize the nip-ups in my stomach. Who would be poking at Vivian Frayne's lock in the middle of the night? And whoever it was—it was taking him a hell of a long time. I waited, panting through an open mouth, feeling the perspiration bristle against my skin. I waited. . . .

Finally the door swung open. And closed.

Somebody was feeling for the light switch.

Somebody brushed against me. I sprang.

We went to the floor together but it was a quick struggle. Once I felt the pick of a sharp instrument against my cheek, but I rolled from it, lashed out twice, and there was no more resistance. We lay still, with me on top, the body beneath me soft and warm. I pushed up, found the light switch, flicked it, and there sprawled supine but always attractive lay Sophia Sierra, not unconscious, her eyes fluttering, surprise still a mark on her face. Her right hand held a sharp-

pronged pick-lock. A black velvet short coat was over the
red dress. A pocketbook was hooked over her shoulder.

She blinked until, it appeared, I came into focus, for,
immediately, she sat up. "You!" she said and that molehill
of a word carried mountains of unspoken rhetoric.

"You!" I replied. "I'll be a son of a bitch!"

"You are," she said and sat and rubbed at her jaw.

"What the hell are you doing here?" I said. I helped her
up. "And with a professional pick-lock yet." She shook her
head groggily, but then she smiled, and I went soft all over
again. "What *are* you doing here?" I said but I said it much
more pleasantly.

"You first," she said. "You tell me first."

We went together to the living room. I put on the light.
She slid the pocketbook down her arm, doffed the black
coat and spilled out on the couch. She looked tired and
frightened but it detracted not at all from the lustre of her
allure. Here we were, in the middle of the night, alone in
an apartment where there was no prospect of our being
disturbed, a frightened girl and a guy very much on the
make—the thing was rife with radiant possibilities: so I
shrugged it off. (I'm sick.)

"Honey," I said. "I'm working."

"Boy, that's all you do, don't you?"

I sat near her, enjoying the warmth of her thigh. "Honey,"
I said, "you're a nice, sweet, attractive gal, and I'm crazy
about you."

"Yeah, I remember," she said.

"So what's with a pick-lock?" I said.

"What?"

"The thing you're holding in your hand."

She looked at it, opened her bag, dropped it into her bag.

"Just a minute," I said. The bag was still open. I fumbled
in my pockets and found a hundred dollar bill. "Yours," I
said. "Something I've been holding for you. From Feninton
for young love out of Las Vegas."

"What are you talking about?" she said.

(Score another against Gordon Phelps who said this was
a slick chick whose one interest in life was loot.)

"A gift from Feninton, remember?" I said. "It's been a
rather interrupted evening, but don't you remember?"

"Oh, yes, that," she said. "But that was a gift for you,
wasn't it, not for me."

"Quiet!" I said and stuffed the bill into her bag. "Now what's with pick-locks?"

"You first," she said. She closed the bag and put it aside. *"You're* supposed to tell *me* what you're doing here."

"You set up the protocol, huh?" My sigh was part fatigue, part lust. "All right, your protocol. I'm here because I'm working on a murder thing, and I'm working in co-operation with the cops."

"Cops?" she said.

"You heard me. I'm here because the cops gave me permission to be here. In fact, they gave me the keys to get in here. You—you're here by virtue of a pick-lock. You've broken in here and you're trespassing. That's a crime either way. If I call the cops in—which, of course, I should do—you're in deep trouble right up to that gorgeous chin of yours. Is that what you want me to do?"

"No," she said.

"Then you're going to have to talk it up, sweetie."

The dark eyes swept over me. I ducked from meeting them. I kept looking at her forehead. "What's with pick-locks?" I said. "Where'd you get it?"

"There are all kinds of guys come into the Nirvana. I had one of them get it for me."

"So you could break your way in here?"

"Yes, that's right," she said.

"Why?" I said.

She bent her head. She primped at her hair. She clicked a fingernail against her teeth. It took time. She was wrestling with a problem, and she finally decided it. In my favor.

"I'll tell you," she said.

I was not in the mood for her favors. Not now.

"You'd better," I said.

She disregarded that. She sat up and crossed her legs. I tried.

"That Vivian Frayne was a crazy bastard," she said.

"Yes, yes, I know all about that. She was good, but she was also bad, and all the rest of that crap. Now, please, let's get to the point. What are you doing here?"

"I might be jammed in her murder."

"Did you do it?"

"No."

"What are you doing here?"

"I'll tell you, if you'll let me."

"I'm trying to let you," I said.

"Phelps wasn't the first guy she'd pinched right from under my nose—"

"Maybe you're too aggressive—"

"I was burning when it happened—"

"So I've heard."

"I beat it out of the Nirvana at that time. I took off for a couple of weeks. I went for a vacation. Matter of fact, I went to Cuba. But I was burning at that Frayne, burning. And when I burn, mister, I burn."

"I hope so," I said.

"I wrote her a few letters from Cuba, three letters to be exact. I told her what I thought of her and her tactics. I told her I'd even it up, one way or another. I told her I had friends, real bad boys, and I told her I was going to see to it that she'd get paid off—in spades. I told her that that pretty face of hers was going to be mashed up, maybe even worse was going to happen to her. I was hot then, burning. I wanted to put a scare into her, and I did. She was scared witless."

"How do you know?"

"She told me, when I got back. First she tried to soft-soap me on the Phelps deal, said it wasn't her fault, that she hadn't made any pitch for him, that he'd just kind of gravitated to her."

"Did you believe it?"

"I did not. She was a liar, and she knew that I knew she was a liar. But by then I was kind of cooled down. I figured that Phelps had kind of passed on me. When some-body's stuck on me, *really* stuck, nobody can drag him off, but *nobody*, not even a Vivian Frayne."

"Did you kind of put a little pressure on him?"

She disregarded that. "So, I figured, if it wouldn't have been Vivian, it would have been somebody else. I knew she was lying, but kind of, I just didn't hold it against her any more. Live and let live and the hell with it."

"This your version now—for the record?"

"Meaning?"

"Your version now—after she's been knocked off?"

"I'm telling you the truth."

"All right. What's that got to do with her being scared witless?"

"She said something else to me, back there at the beginning, when I got back from my vacation. She said that if anything ever happened to her, the cops would know that it came from me, *if* it came from me."

"And how would they know?"

"She said she was saving my letters. She said she was hanging on to them. She said that if anything happened to her, the cops would get those letters, and they'd know I was behind whatever happened to her."

"I get it," I said. "And how'd you feel about that?"

"Once I cooled off, I didn't care. I wasn't going to do anything, I wasn't going to call in any of the bad boys, so I didn't care. I was glad that I had put a little scare into her, that she wouldn't be pulling her tricks on me, that she'd be a little careful in the future—and that was that. I practically forgot about it. We kind of became pretty good friends after that, as a matter of fact. I think you can figure the rest."

"You mean," I said, "you came here tonight hoping to find those letters?"

"That's why I came here."

"So that there wouldn't be any heat on you—for her murder?"

"Sure. Who needs it? You know how cops can push a girl like me around."

"Well, maybe I can take the heat off you—without those letters."

"Like how?" she said.

"If you were working last night, if you were at the Nirvana Ballroom at one o'clock last night—you're a hundred percent in the clear—letters or no letters."

"I wasn't working last night."

"Took the night off? Had a date? Fine. That can be proven too, you know."

"I took the night off but I didn't have a date. I was tired. I stayed home."

"With whom?"

"Alone."

"Stinks," I said. "Leaves you wide open. She was killed last night at about one o'clock."

"Please." She stood up. "Please let me try. Let me look for those goddamned letters."

"Forget it," I said.

"Please!"

"They're not here."

"What are you talking about?"

"Honey, I know from the horse's mouth. They're not here, that's what I'm talking about."

"How the hell would you know?"

"I know—from the horse's mouth."

"What horse?"

"Cops. They've looked this joint over from top to bottom. Minutely, and in force. You couldn't do that kind of search if you had this apartment all to yourself for the next year. Simply," I said, "your letters weren't here."

"But how would you *know?*" It was almost a wail.

"*You'd* know," I said.

"What in all hell are you trying to say?"

This girl was as swear-provoking as a stubbed toe. I did not swear. I rendered it as pontifically as I could manage. "Honey," I said slowly and distinctly, "the cops racked up this joint pretty good. If your letters would have been here, they would have found your letters. And if they would have found your letters, they would have yanked you downtown, and they would probably still have you sitting on your pretty little ass, answering their pretty little questions. Do I, if you please, make myself clear?"

"Yes, yes, you do."

I had been fighting hard but right then I lost the battle. In her despair she was wriggling, and wriggling in that red dress she wore created irresistible impulses within me. So, I did not resist. I went to her and gathered her in.

She fought me off.

"Be nice," I said, my arms around her.

"There's a time to be nice," she said.

"Sorry," I said. "You're so right." I went away from her. "So far you've been right all the way down the line," I said. "I think you're a smart girl, very smart. Maybe you're still being smart right now. Maybe you're making character for yourself right this minute—"

"Please be on my side," she said, all little-girl suddenly.

"Look," I said, "did Vivian Frayne have a vault, do you know?"

"I know she didn't."

"How do you know she didn't?"

"I was curious."

"Why?"

"Because of my letters."

"So how do you know she didn't?"

"I had it checked. By experts. Real experts. Friends who know how to check that sort of thing. You can depend on that. No vault. Not in any bank in the entire city of New York."

"Fits," I said, "because the policy was here and not in a vault."

"What policy?"

"Keep your mind on your own business, will you, sweet?" And then a hunch uncoiled and sprang at me like an outraged husband at a discovered lover. I snapped my fingers. "You know something," I said. "If she saved your letters, I think I know where they are."

"Do you?" she said and she came near and she was suddenly as smooth as yeast, and of similar propensity. "Help me," she said. "Please help me. I'm scared. I admit it. A little bit, I'm scared."

I backed off. "You want to do a little business?"

"Business with you? Of course." She was coy now.

"You want to stop being a liar?"

"Liar! Now what—"

"I'll try for your letters—if you'll stop being a liar."

"I'm telling the truth, you damned—"

"About Mousie Lawrence?"

"Mousie Lawrence?" she said. "I never heard of a—"

"The picture I showed you? Back there at the Nirvana?"

"Oh." She sucked in her breath.

"You were lying about that, weren't you?"

"Yes, but only because I didn't want to talk about what isn't my business. You said I was smart, well, maybe kids like me learn early, we learn to keep our noses clean."

"Start getting it dirty, my love."

"About . . . Mousie Lawrence?"

"About . . . Mousie Lawrence."

"I never heard that name in my life—before you sprang it on me."

"Okay, you never heard that name in your life. But you damn well recognized that picture I showed you."

She was silent.

"Did you?" I said.

"Yes," she said.

"Okay, let's have it."

She was silent.

"Baby," I said, "you're jammed on this deal. I told you I was working with the cops. If I open up, you're *very* jammed."

"You won't. Please."

"I won't, only because I want to get together with you, because I've got a thing going for you, and I'm not especially proud of myself for that. Maybe I wouldn't even open up if I were certain you'd hung this thing on Vivian. There are all kinds of chumps——"

"No, you're not, no."

"But if I did open up, oh sister, you'd be so very jammed. You're wide open on one o'clock last night, you've admitted threatening letters, maybe there are even other reasons why you'd have liked to knock her off, plus your breaking and entering into here with a criminal instrument——sister, you'd be so very jammed, if I opened up——"

"I know, I know, but you won't, please."

"On the other hand, so far you've been the complete clam with me, and I've been the complete chump. How's about trying to be a little fair? How's about showing a little appreciation? I'm way out on the limb——for you."

She strode about the room. I watched her, enjoying every nuance of movement. She went to the couch and sat down and studied her knees. Then she looked up with a tiny, peculiar, guilty little smile, like mama looking up from the pleasure of a comic book and finding junior glaring down at her.

"Yes, I want to be fair," she said. "I want to be fair. What is it? What do you want to know about the man whose picture you showed me?"

"Do you know him?"

"I don't know him as Mousie Lawrence."

"You know him by any other name?"

"Manny Larson."

"Fine," I said. "Where do you know him from?"

"The Nirvana."

"My God," I said, "it's like pulling teeth. Let's have it. Come on, let's have it."

"There was another guy," she said.

"Kiddy Malone? Kenneth Masters?"

"Masters. That's it. Kenny Masters. A little guy too, with a kind of red face."

"All right, all right, let's have it."

"They were picking out girls, kind of picking out special girls, girls who wanted to make a little extra loot, girls who knew how to keep their noses clean, girls who would kind of work a little racket without worrying too much about it."

"What kind of racket?"

"I'm not sure."

"Did they approach you?"

"Yes."

"Did they make the proposition?"

"Yes."

"Did you accept?"

"No."

"What proposition?"

"Simple. I would be given a few packages, oh, a few small packages, no bigger than a couple of lumps of sugar, no bigger than that."

"Who would give them to you? Where?"

"They'd be given to me at home, a man would deliver them. Then, at the dance hall, sooner or later, a man would be dancing with me and he would say, 'I come from Larson.' And I was supposed to say, 'Who's Larson?' And he was supposed to say, 'A friend of Masters.' Then, while we were dancing, I was supposed to slip him the little packet and he was supposed to slip me a folded hundred dollar bill. Somebody, later on, would come to my home to collect. Either I had all the packets, or I had hundred dollar bills for the packets I didn't have. I'd get five bucks for every transaction. Could happen two-three times a night, they told me."

"Why didn't you make the deal?"

"Because it was penny-ante."

"Didn't you also figure it for trouble?"

"I did, but they explained that it couldn't actually be trouble."

"How not, my lass?"

"If anything happened, they said, I was just to tell the truth. A man had come to me with a package, I hadn't known what was in the package, and somebody had paid me for it, and I had delivered the money to someone who had called for it."

"Innocent-pawn-type deal. It could be a little trouble,

but it couldn't be big trouble. What about the delivery guys and the pickup guys?"

"They told me the men would constantly be changed up, and if one of them happened to get caught up with—nobody would blame me. On the other hand, I was to keep my nose strictly clean. If I talked it up, the least that would happen to me would be a dose of acid in my eyes."

"Pretty," I said. "Real pretty."

"What?" she said. She was being coy again.

"They set up a dope-drop in a dance hall," I said. "It's all quiet and furtive in there anyway. They pick special girls who know enough not to shoot their faces off. They use stooges for delivery and pickups. A girl has two-three transactions a night. They pick twenty girls, and they're doing a minimum gross business of four thousand bucks a night, which is approximately twenty-five thousand bucks a week. Given a little luck—once the thing shapes up—it runs a year. That's over a million dollars worth of business, just in one year. Could be much more than that. Could run more than a year. Could use more than twenty girls, could use fifty. Could step up the amount of transactions a night to five or six. Those figures could run up fast to real heavy millions. Fantastic, out of one lousy little dance hall in New York. And the guys who set it up would be in the clear. There'd be layers and layers of in-between nobodies who would take the rap once the thing bust. How about Steve Pedi? Did he talk to you about this?"

"No."

"Did he know what was going on?"

"I don't know."

"Didn't you talk to him about it?"

"No."

"Why not?"

"I was afraid to talk to anybody. They warned me what would happen if I discussed it. I wasn't going out of my way looking for trouble. It was take it or leave it. I left it."

"And the racket's been working? Going on right now?"

"Yes, I'm pretty sure. Since they talked to me, I've kind of been watching. It's hardly noticeable, no one would notice unless they were actually watching hard for it, but I'm pretty sure it's been going on."

"Okay," I said, "thanks a big bunch. Now get up, and let's get out of here." I started putting out the lights.

She stood up, pushed into the black coat, lifted her bag. "My letters . . .?" she said.

"Always there's letters, aren't there? It wouldn't be a murder case without letters. It's like espionage without The Plans, or The Papers, or The Formula." I took her hand. "Come on," I said. "Let's go try for The Letters."

TWENTY-ONE

And so once more I was on my white charger which in this case was a yellow cab and we tooled through the New York night, Sophia Sierra and I, close and comfy, true enough, but as primly conservative as though we were seated in a church pew. And at 11 Charles Street, I paid the cabbie and waited until he tilted his clock and then I laid an additional two dollars in his palm. "Please wait," I said. "You'll have another customer in a few minutes."

"Thanks," he said.

"Will you wait?"

"You bet I'll wait, boss. If it's another customer tips like you, I'm happy. But how'll I know it's *your* customer?"

"He'll say that Larson sent him."

"Good enough, Mr. Larson."

"Very funny," Sophia said as we entered the vestibule. "I suppose a cockeyed sense of humor is better than no sense of humor at all."

"I suppose," I said and pushed the Phillips' button, five short pushes, a pause, and then one long push.

The clicker clicked back faster than the goodnight kiss of a disappointed date. Upstairs, after the peekhole routine, Gordon Phelps opened the door for us. He cast a glance at Sophia and then a quick one back at me.

"Hi, sucker," he said.

"I bring you a guest," I said.

"I notice," he said. "The sulphuric Sophia. You just won't listen to an old man's advice, will you?"

"What advice?" Sophia said.

"An old man's advice based on an old man's experience," I said.

"You guys are nuts," she said.

"Sophia," I said, "would you please go into the bedroom, and please close the door behind you?"

"Bedroom?" she said. "Me?"

"And what could be more appropriate?" Gordon Phelps said.

"The hell with both of you," she said, but she went though she slammed the door viciously.

Gordon Phelps was wearing expensive slacks and a white silk sport shirt. He tried to act chipper but the strain was beginning to show on him. He was pale, satchels bulged beneath his eyes, and he kept chewing on his lower lip as though he were trying to pry loose a piece of stuck cigarette paper.

"Any news?" he said.

"Plenty," I said.

"I'm dying," he said.

"You look it," I said.

"Never mind the comments," he said, "I'm dying to hear."

"The cops are very anxious for you."

"As Sophia would say—the hell with them."

"They've got reason to be anxious. Special reason."

"Special? Why—"

"Vivian Frayne was murdered with bullets shot out of a gun that belongs to you. That's definite. On the line. No question."

"My gun?"

"Your gun, Mr. Phelps. And if you're not the guy that used it, I suggest you turn yourself in."

"Now look here," he said. "I didn't pay you a fee for you to tell me to turn myself in."

"I'm working, Mr. Phelps, believe me. And I'm going to keep on working right through this night. But if I don't come up with something, I suggest you let me bring you in."

"Now, look!" he said.

"You look," I said. "You claim you didn't kill her."

"I didn't."

"You claim you're worried about stuff that may hit the papers."

"Yes, that's right."

"Then listen. The guy in charge of this deal is a good friend of mine, a Detective Lieutenant Louis Parker. He's not a little guy with a big badge. He's a human being. You notice that it's not been splashed all over the papers that that chick got it from your gun——"

"I *gave* her that gun——"

"I know. She had burglars." His eyes opened in a show of respect. He began to realize that I *had* been working. "I don't mean she had burglars," I said, "but she was afraid of burglars, there had been burglars in the apartment house. All right. *I* know that, but Parker doesn't. Do you see what I mean?"

"Not quite."

"He's not a guy to look to ruin a reputation by wild accusations to the newspapers, that's what I mean. There *are* cops like that——*they* get publicity by shooting sensational things at the newspapers. Not Parker. Parker's a human being."

Phelps creased his eyebrows together. "What are you trying to say?"

"I'm trying to say that by tomorrow, Parker will give his stuff to the newspapers, and legitimately so. By tomorrow, you're a fugitive, whether innocent or not. By tomorrow, it'll be public knowledge that Vivian Frayne was killed by a gun owned by Gordon Phelps and that Gordon Phelps has disappeared. Now that's *just* the kind of publicity you want to avoid. Do you follow me, Mr. Phelps?"

He reached for a chair and sank into it slowly. Suddenly he was an old man and his problems were showing. Miserably he said, "I follow you."

"Now when I take you in," I said, "I'll explain the whole bit to Parker, how you hired me, why you hired me, the whole bit. Parker will understand——you're lucky that the guy in charge is Lieutenant Parker. Now, they may hold you, I'm not saying they won't. If you're telling the truth, then they may hold you as a material witness. If you don't raise a stink and start screaming for a lawyer, they'll probably put you up at a hotel, and the papers won't have a word about it. Oh, they'll question you, they'll shove you through the meat grinder, you can be sure of that."

"Pleasant prospect," he groaned but I could see he was beginning to fall in with the idea.

"If you stay with your story, and there are no real cracks in it—that's all they'll have—your story—and even if you did this thing—and you stay with your story—that's no proof of murder. You might get deeper into the jam jar, but you're right deep in it at this moment. Look at it from any angle you like, Mr. Phelps—my bringing you in is the right thing. Even if it happens you're tried for this murder, it'll look good for a jury—coming in with me instead of running away—it's coming in voluntarily, not being caught up with as a fugitive."

He got up out of the chair. "Then why don't we go in now, right now?"

"Because I've given myself this night to keep working. Maybe, if I get lucky, I can save you a lot of grief. On the other hand, I may pin it on you a hundred percent. You want to take that chance?"

"Yes," he said.

"Good boy," I said. "Okay, get on your jacket and start getting out of here."

"Out of here? What are you talking about?"

It was time for a bit of fabrication. In my profession, it is called goosing the client. "I'm talking about cops," I said. "They've been doing a lot of checking amongst Vivian's friends. She may have talked out of turn about this little hideaway. Somebody may slip with something, and then they're here, and they've caught up with you, a fugitive in hiding. That will *not* look very good, in the papers, with a jury—anywhere. Now here's what I want you to do."

"What?"

I gave him my address and apartment number, and my keys. "Slip into a jacket and go over to my place. Nobody will be looking for you there, except me. I'll stick around here for a short while. When I go, I'll lock up."

He closed the collar of his sport shirt, went to a closet, unhooked a suburban jacket, and shrugged into it. He was as pale as the belly of a shark. He poked in the pocket of his trousers and produced a leather packet.

"My keys," he said.

"I don't need your keys."

"Then how'll you lock up here?"

"I have Vivian Frayne's keys."

I took them out and jingled them.

He looked as though he were going to faint.

"Where'd you get those keys?" he said.

"From the cops. One of those keys fits here, as you know."

"From the cops?" he said.

"Where else?" I said.

There was a white tinge of fright around his nostrils. "Look, you're not going to railroad me, are you? You're not in cahoots with them?"

"Don't you trust me, Mr. Phelps?"

"In a situation like this, I don't know whom to trust. I've been sitting here, thinking, going crazy all day."

"You didn't kill her, did you?"

"No!"

"Then how can you be railroaded? I'm in cahoots with the cops up to this point—I've told them that I'm working for you, and I've told them that I'd bring you in by this morning. That's the truth. If you call that being railroaded, well then, you're railroaded."

He stared at me for a long time, shrugged, started for the door.

"Call your wife," I said.

"*What?*" He whirled about.

"Your wife," I said. "She's been in town for the past couple of days. She's been reading the papers. She's worried about you."

"How would *you* know?" he said.

"The lady retained me."

"For what?"

"To find you. She paid me a thousand dollars."

His eyes blinked in a frightened squint. "Kind of a crook, aren't you?" he said but he said it mildly. He was worried about me, worried about what he had gotten himself into with me, and he showed it.

"Why a crook?" I said. "The lady can afford it, and if I'd have insisted upon an extra thousand from you, I'd have gotten it, wouldn't I? As a matter of fact, as it turned out, I used that thousand for expenses, and you're not going to have to reimburse me."

"Expenses? For what?"

"For trying to keep you out of the can, if that's possible. Now go keep my hearth warm, Mr. Phelps, and if anybody calls, don't answer. It might be Adam Frick."

That laid an egg.

"Why should Adam Frick call you?" he said.

"He can't, really," I said. "He's dead."

Poor Gordon Phelps. His pallor took on a hue of green. "What? What? What the devil?"

"Murdered in his apartment. You weren't out of here tonight, were you?"

"Go to hell," he said.

"Tell you all about it when I see you later," I said. "Now please run along, Mr. Phelps. You look like you need a rest. Pick out some long-hair records and listen to them on my hi fi. Relax and rest. Either I or Sophia, or both of us, will be back at my apartment pretty soon. We'll use the same system."

"What system?" he said weakly.

"The same as we used here. Five short rings, a pause, then one long one. You get that, you open up. Otherwise, you don't open up, you just stay put."

Once more, he started for the door.

"There's a taxi waiting downstairs," I said.

And once more, he turned to me. "You think of everything, don't you?" Mildly, but slightly sardonically.

"I've been paid to try to think of everything, and you're the fella who paid me, remember? Just tell the taxi guy that Larson sent you."

That laid another egg.

I was watching his face. Nothing happened to his face.

"Ever hear of Larson?" I said. "Manny Larson?"

"No," he said.

"Okay, just tell him Larson sent you anyway. Good-bye, Mr. Phelps. Good luck."

He either had an iron control, which was possible, or he used fright as a disguise, which was possible; or he knew nothing of the deaths of Mousie Lawrence and Adam Frick, which was just as possible.

What did he know of the death of Vivian Frayne?

TWENTY-TWO

Gordon Phelps departed with a mild click of the door-
lock and immediately I routed Sophia out of the bedroom,
a procedure precisely the reverse of my inclinations toward
Sophia, but business is business and bedrooms can wait, and
all damned night long it had been business.

"Take off the coat, kid," I said. "Make yourself comfortable."

She took off the coat and made herself comfortable. At
once, of course, I became uncomfortable. "Now please," I
said, "according to you, Vivian Frayne did not have a bank
vault, and according to me she couldn't have had your
letters in her apartment."

Demurely Sophia Sierra said, "We covered that territory,
remember?"

"On the other hand," I said, "she did have a key to this
place, and she was free to come here—even while Phelps was
away on trips, vacations, that sort of thing."

"How do you know?"

"Phelps told me. So, what do you think about here, right
here, for the spot to look for buried treasure?"

"I think you're a very bright guy, Mr. Chambers."

I bowed, modestly, like an actor taking a curtain call, but
I went after more applause because applause from Sophia was
salve to my psyche. "I don't think she even trusted Phelps on
that deal."

"Now how do you come to that conclusion, Mr. Sherlock?"

"I don't think she'd want anything in *his* hands—that *you*
wanted very much. Like that he might have talked a little
trade with you, so's he could get his hands on you, even if it
would be a one-shot deal." I rubbed at my chin. "I'm certain
Phelps knows nothing."

"Oh, now you're certain."

"If he'd have known about those letters, he would have

produced them for me. Phelps was trying to get out from under, and he frankly didn't care whom he implicated. He told me about the hate you had going for Vivian. If he knew about those letters, he'd have produced them for verification."

"Yeah, yeah," she said breathlessly.

"So if they're here, they're somewhere where Phelps wouldn't be likely to fall over them. That excludes all the usual places. All right. What does it include? I'm in the business of looking for things, and I've found that people just don't have imagination along that line. They're influenced by movies and television, they do the usual ordinary thing, and somehow *they* think they're doing the unusual."

"Like what? I mean, what's usual, what unusual?"

"What would *you* do," I said, "if you were seeking an unusual site for the hiding of an object, I mean something flat like three letters? Of course, you'd exclude desk drawers and places like that. You might think of under the mattress and then you'd dismiss that because people turn their mattresses. Then you'd come up with a bright idea—one of two bright ideas. You'd either Scotch-tape them tightly beneath a piece of furniture, preferably a low, heavy piece; or you'd slit the brown paper back of a picture on a wall, stick them in there, Scotch-tape it intact, and put the picture back on the wall. Am I wrong?"

"You're too damned right, you louse," she said admiringly.

"People go by rote, my sweet. We learn that in my business and we use it, it saves us a lot of time." I looked about. "There's plenty of furniture in this joint, and just one picture, that rose-colored nude up there over the fireplace. Okay," I said. "Let's work as a team. You take the bedroom, I'll do here."

"Always the bedroom," she said, just a mite mockingly.

"But where else, my beloved?" I said.

I marched her to the bedroom and put her to work. In the living room I had myself a drink and then I sneaked to the bedroom door and peeked. That gorgeous figure stretched on the floor wriggling about was something to see. I had to tear myself away but tear I did. I went for the rose-colored nude before I went for the furniture perhaps because I'm more attracted to rose-colored nudes than to furniture, and sure enough, first crack, there was Scotch-tape on the brown paper back. I worked fast, ripped open the back, and pried out three letters complete with envelopes. They were all addressed to

Vivian Frayne, all postmarked Cuba, all in one handwriting, feminine and flowery. But I pried out an additional envelope, a legal-sized envelope, unaddressed, blank, but sealed and somewhat bulky. I opened that quickly. It contained a marriage certificate from Montreal, Canada, expressing connubial sanction for Vivian Jane Frainovitski and Stephan Burton Pedi. It was dated four years ago. The envelope contained one other document: a certificate of divorce from a court in Montreal, Canada, dissolving this selfsame marriage between Vivian Jane Frainovitski and Stephan Burton Pedi. It was dated four months ago. I replaced the documents in the envelope and stuck that into my pocket. Then I restored the rose-colored nude to the wall and, with three envelopes in my hand, went to the bedroom and lounged against the door jamb, watching the undulations of a long-curved body crawling about a carpeted floor seeking beneath furniture. I enjoyed for a while and then I said: "These the letters?"

She did not hear me. Her head was beneath the bed at that moment: only legs, rump and torso were exposed. I enjoyed some more.

"These the letters?" I said after a while, more loudly.

She came out from beneath the bed. (Near the bed, beneath the bed, but never *in* the bed.) She stood up, dusting herself. She was very beautiful, flushed, eyes ablaze, a smudge on one cheek.

"What?" she said.

"These the letters?" I waved them.

She came in a hurry. She looked at the envelopes in my hand. "Yes," she said. "All three?"

"All three," I said.

"Gimme."

I moved away. "Easy," I said.

She moved after me. "Gimme," she said. "Please."

"Not yet," I said.

"When?"

"Not yet," I said.

A pleasantly crafty look crept into her eyes, a feminine look, pleasant to the male; a filmed, narrow, seductive look; a look with a little smile about the eyes. Her lips came to mine and opened softly against my opening mouth. I stood as though rooted, savoring her; her arms tightly around me, my arms behind my back.

That is a lousy way to make love.

She released me, moved back, seemed shy. "Gimme," she said softly.

I swallowed to find voice.

"Not yet," I croaked.

"Why?" Her hands flung up. "Goddamn you, why?"

I went to the living room and she followed.

"Sweetie," I said, "you're going to have to string along with me. I can't turn anything over to anybody before I get this damned thing straightened out. Believe me, I want to, but even if I want to, I can't. Crazy?"

"And how."

"I suppose you've got to be a man," I said seriously, "to be able to understand. With a man there's work and there's love, and I hate to get off on this philosophical kick, but that's the way it is, work and love, and, sooner or later, when a man is truly put to the test, his work is Number One. Love can't interfere with work, and even this . . . this thing between us, the cockeyed thing between us which may be love—it can't interfere with work. I'll see you through on this bit, I'll do my best for you, I'm all the way on your side, but I'm not turning anything over to anyone, not until this thing is cleared up and wrapped away. That's my work," I said stubbornly.

Somehow it got through.

Her shoulders, which were up stiffly, sagged.

She took up her bag, went for her coat, lifted it by its collar, threw it over one shoulder like a knapsack.

"What do you want me to do?" she said quietly.

"Go to my place and wait for me."

"All right. I'll go."

"Phelps is there."

"Phelps?"

"You two ought to spend an interesting evening together." I grinned. "You ring five short rings, wait a second, then one long one. Do that, and he'll open up for you."

"You coming?"

"I'm leaving here with you. I'll put you in a cab."

"Can't you come with me?"

"I wish I could."

"Where you going?"

"Maybe to get killed," I said.

TWENTY-THREE

I got her a cab and got me another. I sat and sifted it around in my head as I was driven toward 244 West 65th Street. I had it, I had most of it: a lot depended on Kenny Masters, born Malone, alias Kiddy. I sifted it around, and I liked what I had.

The street was quiet and desolate, very dark near 244. The cabbie pulled away as soon as he was paid, and I was alone. I shuddered once and violently, although it was not cold, and then I entered a vestibule that was dim and blue-like under one thin fluorescent. The stoolie-genius was correct again: the entrance door opened to a push. The hallway was airless, dank with an old smell of cooked fish. I climbed to the first floor, leaning on a creaking bannister that was as weak as an alliance between enemies. I went to the rear apartment on the right. There was no bell. Dried paint crusted from the top of an old green door. I stood in front of the door for a long moment, rubbing my lips against my teeth. Then I knocked.

There was no answer.

I knocked again.

And again and again.

I was worried that I might wake a neighbor, but I kept knocking, rapping softly but continuously. At long last there was a sound from within: footsteps: a soft barefoot patter. I stopped knocking. The muted sounds ceased.

I knocked again. Once. Hard.

"Yes?"

It was a woman's voice, soft-pitched. She was in darkness —no light showed in the slit beneath the door.

"Yes?" she said. "What is it? Who is it?"

I put my mouth close.

"Open up," I said.

"Who is it? What do you want?"

We were speaking in whispers.

"I want Kiddy Malone," I said urgently. "Open up."

"There's no Kiddy Malone here."

"You want cops, lady?"

There was no answer.

"I'm a friend," I said. "I'm a friend of Kiddy."

"Who are you?"

"Tell him Pete Chambers. Tell him quick."

Silence. Then the shuffle of the bare feet.

I leaned my forehead against the door. When I moved it back I saw the dark stain of my perspiration. I took out my handkerchief and wiped my face. I put it back and touched myself, almost involuntarily, touching for a gun. I had no gun on my person. I wished I did have. Then again, perhaps it was better that I didn't. A cokey is a tricky individual to cope with. You cannot predict his mood. Perhaps an approach with a gun would frighten him. I waited, wanting to use the handkerchief again, but I did not. I stood rigid, leaning against the door, waiting.

It seemed a long time before I heard her again. This time it was the tap-tap of high heels. I moved from the door and braced myself. She was going to open up, otherwise she would not have put her shoes on. A woman is a woman: a woman does not open the door to a stranger when she is barefoot. She had also probably primped a bit, which is why she had taken so long. A woman is a woman.

I heard a click.

A strip of light appeared beneath the door.

"Are you there?" she whispered.

"Right here," I said.

I heard a bolt pull away. The door opened wide and I entered directly into a living room. I did not see the woman. She had remained behind the door as I had entered. Now the door closed and I heard the bolt shoot back into place. I still did not see the woman. She was behind me and I did not turn. I saw Kiddy Malone and that is why I did not turn.

He was seated in an armchair, squarely in the middle of the room, facing me. His hair was tousled but his face was clean and shaven. He was wearing expensive, tight-fitting, yellow silk pajamas of the ski type. He was smiling but it was stiff: it seemed to be carved on his face. But his eyes were good, better than I had expected. He had stuff in him, but he had it right: he was not overloaded, nor was he in need of a jolt. His blue Irish eyes were clear, the pupils not too widely distended. That pleased me. And his hands were steady, which pleased me even more, because one hand was holding a huge automatic.

"Hi, Kiddy," I said.

"What do you want?" he said.

His voice was good too. I was in luck. I began to relax. I stopped sweating.

"That the way to greet a friend?" I tried for a gay voice. It came out slightly falsetto.

He seemed ashamed. His smile became more real, less rigid. "It's a pretty lousy time to come calling, ain't it?"

"It's because it's important, Kiddy boy. I come as a friend and"—I gestured toward his gun—"look how you greet me."

"You heeled?" he said.

"Would I come heeled—to a friend?"

"Feel my friend, Betty."

I finally saw her. Once again the stoolie-genius was correct. She was a redhead with a sensational shape, built for a stripper rather than a waitress. She was tall—probably a head taller than Kiddy—with a full large powerful figure, and friend Kiddy had done well for her in the matter of night clothes. She was wearing white silk high-heeled lounging shoes and a white silk tight-mesh negligee, practically transparent. She had huge upright breasts and a roundly convex graceful rump. Long full thighs glistened in the silk as she moved toward me. Unfortunately, there was a disconcerting note, disconcertingly similar to Kiddy Malone's disconcerting note.

She too was holding a gun.

Naturally, he was not as bright as he thought he was. If I were on a rash errand, her coming like that to frisk me would have been a godsend. I could have clipped her gun, used her as a shield, and taken my chances. But I was not being rash this trip. I stood meek as a frightened patient behind a fluoroscope. She felt me.

"No gun," she said.

His smile contracted to penitent pursed lips.

"Sorry, fella," he said.

"I come as a friend," I said. I wanted to hammer that through.

His gun was no longer pointed at me. It rested, within the grip of his hand, in his lap. He looked like a mischievous little boy caught holding the matches with which he was going to set fire to the kitchen.

"Give my friend a drink, Betty," he said. "He drinks Scotch, the best in the house."

Kiddy Malone was in good shape. I was delighted.

"You're in good shape," I said.

"The best," he said. "Sit down, friend. Make yourself to home."

I sat on one end of a divan. The redhead had disappeared into another room, but she came back quickly, without the gun, but with a tray on which was a bottle of Scotch, an open bottle of soda, a pitcher of water, and glasses.

"If you want ice . . . ?" she began.

"Oh, no, thank you. This is fine."

She set the tray down near me, and she sat herself down on the other end of the divan.

"How do you like my Betty?" Kiddy said.

"A beautiful lady," I said.

"Thank you," she said and she smiled with strong white teeth. She had a wide high-boned face and round blue eyes.

"She's the greatest," Kiddy said. "Big as she is, she's really little. The smallest, believe me, she's really the smallest." He laughed loudly and in the middle of it he suddenly stopped laughing and frowned. "What brings you, Petie? What they call an ungodly hour. What brings you?" And now the carved smile was on his face again, and it was a frightened smile. "And how the hell did you know to get here?" His eyes darted to Betty and back to me.

I poured Scotch and gulped it raw. I needed it.

"I found you," I said, "because you're in trouble. When you're in trouble, that's when a friend is supposed to find you."

"He's a friend," he said to Betty, nodding seriously, but the carved smile remained.

I looked about the room. It was plainly furnished. The floor was bare.

"Not quite like the Montrose," I said, "eh, Mr. Masters?"

The smile dissolved. The gun popped up again.

"Please don't point that thing at me, Kiddy," I said. "I'm on your side. I'm with you."

"What the hell goes?"

"Did you pop him?"

"Me? You out of your brains?" Then his eyes grew crafty.
"Pop who?" he said.

"Mousie Lawrence had most of his face shot away. Both
your holsters were there in the bedroom. Yet you've got a
piece right here in your hand. That what you shot him with,
Kiddy?"

"Not me. You're out of your brains. Why should I pop
Mousie? Mousie's my partner."

"Was," I corrected.

"Mousie was my partner."

"Then what about the gun you're holding?"

"I kept two pieces here, two spare pieces. The one the
lady's got, and this one. Kept them here. Kept a load of
junk here too. Kiddy's no dope, man."

"Kiddy, you in shape?" I said.

"The best," he said.

"Tell me true," I said.

"The best," he said.

"Did you blast Mousie?"

"No."

"Because if you did, I'm the boy to cover you up, and
you know it. Did you, Kiddy boy?"

"No . . . no. No! You hear me, you bastard! No!"

Kiddy Malone did not kill Mousie Lawrence.

I had my story. Complete.

Now it was up to him.

"Okay," I said. "I've got it straight."

"Got what straight?"

"I know the deal. And I can pull you through. But you've
got to work with me, kid, you've got to work *with* me."

The gun was back in his lap. His hands were clenched over
it. "You know shit, pal," he said. "You don't know no deal.
You're trying to shake up a buck. You don't know nothing.
You're a talker. You're trying to shake up a buck, that's what
you're doing. Trying to talk your way into a fancy buck.
Okay, talk. Mabe you will talk yourself into some fancy
bucks."

"I don't want to shake up any bucks. Not from you, Kiddy."

"Then what the hell do you want?"

"I want to pull you out of it, Kiddy. You're practically a
dead man, Kiddy. You know that. Down deep, you know
that. We're old friends, Kiddy, I know you and you know
me. You're just sitting here waiting to get killed. Oh, you've

got a gun in your hands, and you may make it tough for them, but you're just sitting here waiting to get killed, and you know it."

He stared at me for a long time. Then, without any change in expression, he began to cry. The tears came out of the inner corners of his eyes and ran down his nose. He made no effort to wipe them. He sniffed, once.

"Okay, Betty," he said. "Get out of here."

She stood up. "I think he is a friend," she said.

"Get out of here."

She smiled at me. "I really think you are. I hope you can help him. He's a good guy."

"Yes," I said, "he's a good guy."

"Excuse me," she said. "I'll go to sleep now."

"Yeah, go to sleep, baby," Kiddy said. "The stuff you got in you, you'll sleep real good, real good. Good night, baby."

She went away, and I watched her going away, and I enjoyed watching her go away. She closed the door of the other room behind her.

"Give," Kiddy said. "Let's hear. Let's hear the deal, baby boy. Talk it up for me, sweetie boy."

"I'll talk. You listen. You're in shape, you said."

"The best. Talk. I'm listening."

"We start at the start," I said, and then I threw in a threat. "By the way, what I know, the cops know. I may fling a guess here and there—but the cops, they've got it all nice and clean."

"Talk, baby. Kiddy's listening."

I drew a deep breath. "You and Mousie," I said, "came into town to set up the Nirvana. Sweet deal too. Package stuff, passed through some of the smart chicks, at a hundred bucks a throw."

His eyes widened. He nodded. He was mystified but he was approving of me.

"Steve Pedi was in on the pitch . . ." I threw it and let it lie. He smiled, nodding: he still approved of me.

I had it all. It was complete.

"Steve Pedi," I said, "was in on the pitch, although he would deny it if it ever shaped up trouble. He just didn't know a thing that was happening to his girls—if it shaped up trouble. Like that—if it shaped up trouble—the most that could happen to him would be a revocation of his dance hall license."

"It didn't figure to shape up trouble," Kiddy said.

"Of course not," I said. "That was his end, Pedi's end—the local end. With a little political pressure, a little bit of ice spread in the right places—this thing could run and run. You guys were here to set it up, to get it running, and it was just beginning to go—when a crazy dame butts her nose in. Vivian Frayne. Somehow, she got wind of what was cooking—maybe one of the chicks there let it bleed a little—and this Frayne is nuts in the mother-hen department. She gets to Steve and threatens to blow the whistle unless the operation is cut off quick."

"Crazy dame, huh? Boy, how some dames is crazy."

"Stevie-boy fast-talks her, but she's a dead pigeon from the moment she opened up. Here's a crazy dame that's do-gooding on an operation that can gross millions of bucks. All right. So Stevie calls you guys in. You've got to pop her, and pop her quick. No sense calling in anybody else, because anybody else only widens out a murder clique. Keep it close, figures Stevie-boy, because Stevie-boy is a pretty smart fella. So you guys are going to pop her, and pop her quick, although you're kind of out of practice, you're big shots now. How'm I doing?"

"Keep punching, pal." In his own way, Kiddy was being proud of me.

"He rigged it with you guys," I said, "to make it look like a mugging killing, but it got scrambled and he was boiling. He had to move very fast after that, because if she began to think about it, she might get the angle, and then it would be the whistle but quick. So he made the move himself. Now I'll be telling you things you don't know."

"Tell me, boy," Kiddy said. "You're a brain-guy, I always said so."

"Steve Pedi used to be married to Vivian Frayne. He still had the key to the apartment. He also knew there was a gun in the apartment that belonged to a guy called Phelps who had a grudge against her because she was trying to pull some black dough out of him. That set it up pretty good, if he could lay his hands on that gun. So last night he goes to her apartment, rings the bell, and she's not home yet. He uses his key and goes in. He finds the gun he's looking for, and he hides out, probably on the terrace, until she comes home. She gets into her lounging clothes, he comes out, and pops her with Phelps' gun, which he leaves there. He reminds himself that she must have the marriage certificate, also the divorce decree—because they were married and divorced. So he gives the joint a toss, looking for those documents."

"Why?" Kiddy asked.

"He figures if he can get rid of them, he won't be tied in at all. He'd just be an employer of the chick, period. And there'd be no idea that he might have a key. So he gives the place a search, but he doesn't find either document. Okay, it's not good, but it's not fatal. If the stuff is found, it might tie him in a little, but not too much, unless it gets tied tighter and there are only two guys in the world who can tie it tighter. Get it, pal?"

"I get it, pal."

"You and Mousie."

"I get it, pal."

"Am I giving you any new stuff?" I said.

"A little," he said.

"But you guys didn't know, when he came visiting you at the Montrose, that he had already paid a visit at Vivian's. By the way, he had locked that door from the outside, just to make things look kosher—he'd probably figured Phelps had a key to the place, which Phelps didn't."

"Okay, okay, he's now visiting our place."

"He came with a heater. If he gets rid of you two, he's clean all the way around—completely clean of the murder that you guys messed up in the first place—and the operation keeps going because you guys can be replaced. He's a smart cookie. He had pulled a murder. A smart cookie gets rid of anything—or anyone—that can tie him to murder. You guys can tie him, so he's set to get rid of you. As far as the organization is concerned, he's got a clean beef—you guys tripped up on a murder. You trip, you stink, you're out. You messed a murder and you messed a deal that could go in the millions, plus he's got relatives high in the organization. So whatever he does—he's clean with the boys. Plus he's a hero, because it turns out the cops figured a print on the knife that was dropped, the print was Mousie's, and the cops are out looking for Mousie. You following?"

"I'm getting ahead of you," Kiddy said, but his approval was disappearing; he was growing sad.

"So he comes to the Montrose for a little chatter. He's going to ball you guys out for the miss, and plan a new little deal for Vivian, who is already dead, only you guys don't

know it, it hasn't hit the news yet. He's a friend, practically
the boss in this operation, so your guns are in the bedroom,
and you're all gentlemen. Next, he starts shooting, clips
Mousie." I stopped and I smiled. "Your turn now, Kiddy,"
I said. "Pick it up from there."

"I rammed him," Kiddy blurted. "Gave him the rush, the
head to the belly, and knocked him on his ass. I didn't have
a gun on me, and his gun was in his hand, so I ran. And
here I am, pal." He lifted a hand to his hair and pulled on
it, ruminatively. "You found me," he said. "It figures he'll
find me too."

"So will the cops."

"The hell with them."

"Cops are your salvation, Kiddy."

"Sure, cops are my salvation."

"Wake up, for Chrissake, Kiddy."

"What the hell you talking about?"

"You're in the middle, Kiddy, and you've got no out. It's
not only Pedi who's gunning for you now, it's the whole
organization, because you stink now, you're through. You
messed a murder, you messed a big operation, and you're an
actual eyewitness to murder, Mousie's murder. Witnesses to
murder don't live long when they're on the wrong side of
the organization. You're dead right now, kid, and you know
it, and even if you get out of here, you've got no place to
run, and you know that too. You've got nothing, nobody,
except one friend—me. I can keep you alive, Kiddy."

I had my fingers crossed. He was crying again but I did not
care about that. He either accepted me or he rejected me—
now, right now. The man was a hophead. Which way would
he turn?

"I can keep you alive," I said and I waited.

And then, finally, he said: "How?"

I had him.

"Listen, kid," I said. "Listen hard. You've got no choice.
You're a dead man. The whole organization is after you, and
Pedi is pushing them, because with you alive, *he* can be a
dead man convicted of murder. He killed Mousie, didn't he?
He killed your pal. And you're next. So you've got nothing to
lose by turning around on him, do you understand? I take
you in. I take you in, personally, and you turn around on
him."

"Sure, but what happens to me?"

"Nothing, really. Maybe they won't be able to prove the Frayne murder on him, but they'll prove Mousie, with you as State's witness."

"Sure, but what happens to me?" he insisted.

"Nothing, pal. The best happens to you. You're an alien, an illegal-entry alien. What happens to you—you get deported. The cops figure to work with you. You're turning State's evidence, you're a big wheel, you're important to them. And you're going to spill your guts, everything, the whole deal. For that, there's a hell of a lot of appreciation, believe me. They'll fix you with a bodyguard, they'll even change your name for you, and they'll deport you back to Ireland where you get lost in the shuffle if you don't play the bright spots too hard. Even Mexico can't reach out for you when you're lost somewhere in your own country. After a while, they'll forget about you. Pedi'll have the chair, so he can't press them. And you've got dough, I know that, plenty of dough, stashed away. After a while you'll get it together, and you'll begin to move around. My advice, stick to Europe, stay away from here. Are you listening to me, Kiddy? I'm making a live one out of a dead one. Are you listening?"

"Yeah, I'm listening."

"Do I make sense?"

"God damn right you do."

"I'm glad you were in shape to listen."

"Me too. Lopsided, you might have been a sorry boy for coming here."

"I took my chances, Kiddy."

"Yeah, you took your chances, boy. Why?"

"I wanted to make a live one out of a dead one. I know you a long time, Kiddy."

"Yeah, a long time, boy. Frigged up world, huh?"

"Go get dressed, Kiddy. Right now."

"Yeah, I'll go get dressed," he said. "Right now. Here, hold this."

And he gave me his gun.

TWENTY-FOUR

I brought in Kiddy, and then I brought in Sophia and
Phelps, and Parker's people brought in Steve Pedi. I re-
quested that the cops did not make Phelps' involvement public—there was no need—and they agreed (which earned my
fee). Then I did it big and loud and glorious, mostly to
impress Sophia Sierra. I told them all I knew on Frayne, and
Kiddy told them all he knew on Pedi, which really wrapped
it up, but I also cleared up the Frick bit. Since Vivian had
told Adam, little Adam had finally added it up—the narcotics
situation at Nirvana, the fact that Pedi had been married
to Vivian, the fact that Pedi probably had a key. So he had
tapped Pedi for a conference, but Adam was playing out of
his league, and Pedi had come and blasted him with the
very same gun he had used on Mousie. When I had arrived,
Adam's last gasp of "wife, wife" had been a reference to
Vivian, his dying attempt at a tip-off both to his murderer
and to his murderer's connection with Vivian (although my
interpretation had had to do with another man's wife). I
omitted all reference to Mrs. Barbara Phelps (which assured
me of an interesting client for the future) and I omitted all
reference to Sophia's letters which made me a hero with
Sophia (and there was no one I more wished to be a hero
with). Parker and the District Attorney saw it my way about
trading with Kiddy—his testimony in return for deportation
and good riddance—and so ended a long night.

Or did it begin?

For, at long last, I was back in my apartment, alone with
Sophia Sierra, and we were toasting one another with Rob
Roys (not too sweet), and we were both as tight as the boasts
of a brothel girl, when I returned her letters.

"Oh, lover," she said, "you're wonderful, wonderful. You're
the sweetest, the sweetest. . . ." She threw the letters in the

air, watched them go plop, and reached for me. "I love you," she said.

And this was the girl that old Phelps had described as exclusively on the hunt for loot. Poor old Phelps.

She kissed me and we swayed, clinging to one another, probably to keep from falling down. We were swacked on the Rob Roys, looped like sailors' knots, and we were enjoying every dizzy moment.

"You were wonderful, lover," she said.

"Aahhh," I grunted modestly.

"Wonderful," she said.

"Aahhh," I grunted intelligently.

"You make lots of money," she said, "don't you?"

"Lots, lots, lots," I said.

"Wonderful," she said.

"Aahhh," I said.

I held her tightly. I kissed her warmly.

"Five thousand dollars," she said, "from Mr. Phelps."

"A lousy five thousand," I said.

"Wonderful," she said.

"Aahhh," I said, squeezing her.

"You make many thousands, don't you?"

"Many, many, many," I said.

"You could help a girl like me."

"Sure," I said.

"I want to be an actress. I want to be an actress more than anything else in the world."

"Sure," I said.

"You're wonderful."

"Aahhh," I said.

"Would you help me?"

"Sure," I said, suddenly sober.

"There's a teacher," she said. "Strassan. Elia Strassan. He's retired, but he would take me on, he thinks I have talent. He would take me on, for a year, but he wants a fee in advance."

"Aahhh," I said glumly. "Of course. Advance."

"Ten thousand dollars, lover. Only ten thousand dollars. A man like you, a wonderful man like you, it doesn't really mean anything. But a girl like me, without help, it . . . it's impossible. Will you help me, lover? Please? Will you?"

"Sure," I said as my hands fell from around her. "Sure,

I'll help. Sure, my sweet, my beloved, my true love, my one and only. Sure, sure, sure, sure. . . ."

And so ended my romance with Sophia Sierra.

Before it began.

(Postscript to Gordon Phelps. My humble apologies, sir. A dope is a dope is a dope is a dope, and a cocky big-male dope who derides well-meant advice and is contemptuous of the adviser, that is a real, platinum-edged, fourteen-carat, A-Number-One-type dope. Sir, I am a real, platinum-edged, fourteen-carat, A-Number-One-type dope. Regards to all, be good to your neighbors, be kind to animals, and watch your wife. Love and thistles, yours truly, Peter Chambers.)

Printed in the United States
By Bookmasters